A Rose and a Wolf

JEANNE AMBER SIX

ISBN 978-1-966540-12-0 (softcover)
ISBN 978-1-966540-13-7 (ebook)

This book is a work of fiction. Names, characters, places, and incidents are the product of the author's imagination or are used fictitiously. Any resemblance to actual locales, events, or persons, living or dead, is purely coincidental.

Printed in the United States of America.

A Rose and a Wolf

JEANNE AMBER SIX

This book is dedicated to my husband.
Thank you for all the help and for dealing with my craziness.

Chapter 1

Before Raven was 4, her world seemed to be a lonely and cold place. Her mother seemed to ignore her; her father was rumored to have died in a war with another clan before she was born. The rest of the village of Rain Rock avoided her. The only person that seemed to want her was the herbal woman, Key-Na, who took her in when Raven was four winters old. The few times that Raven saw her mother after Key-Na took her in, it was from a distance. Then when Raven was 5 years old, she no longer saw her mother anywhere in the village and Key-Na never mentioned her again. Raven was convinced that her mother had died.

When Raven was 6 years old, her and Key-Na went into Rain Rock for supplies. While in town Raven had seen some children playing and she went over to play with them. When an elder saw her and yelled at her. Raven didn't say anything she just ran back to Key-Na then on the way home she asked.

"Why do the Elders not like me?" Key-Na responded in a wise voice

"They think you are a witch, because of your unusual hair and eyes. Not everyone has black hair with white stripes running through it. When they look into your eyes, they see how golden brown and soulful they are. All these reasons are why you are unique, and why the elders ostracize you and me. Also, the fact that I let you run wild. You, they ostracize because you are different. Me, they ostracize because I came from somewhere else. Also, I have the ability to heal." After Key-Na was done talking, Raven never asked her again why the villagers didn't like her. Nor did she ever wander off to play with the other children again.

As Raven grew older, she learned about herbs. How to gather them and the best ways dry them from Key-Na. Occasionally on their outings Raven would come across an injured animal, Key-Na and Raven would take it home were Raven would practice her herbal knowledge to heal the animal. Once the animal was healed, she would let it go.

When Key-Na felt that Raven was ready she began to show her how to make the more complex tinctures, and potions; as well as teaching her the more dangerous herbs. During this time Raven was also learning how to read, write, and do her sums. When Raven reached her 16th birthday, Key-Na was having her help with patients; whether they came to Key-Na, or Key-Na and Raven went to them. Raven also was helping Key-Na with birthing in the nearby area and villages. After a year of helping Key-Na Raven took over and only needed Key-Na when there was a hard birth, or a case that Raven had not dealt with before.

The winter of Raven's 19th year she was sadder than she had ever been in her whole life. The reason was because Key-Na died the night of the first snow fall of the year from old age. When Raven went into the village to ask for help burying Key-Na, all the villagers told her.

"We are afraid to touch her; the elders told us that if we were to touch her, her witch powers would transfer to us. Then we would be the devil's minions just like you and her are."

In the end Raven buried Key-Na on her own under a large weeping willow tree, that Key-Na loved. That winter was very hard on Raven. She felt that she was all alone in the world. The snow was so deep that it climbed halfway up the sides of the cottage. With the deep snow, no one came for remedies or to ask for help for any birthing. What else made the winter so hard on her was because, she had no one to talk to, to help her through her despair.

In the spring, when the wildflowers began to bloom, people started to seek out help again. In the evenings, Raven would pick some flowers and walk to Key-Na's grave. She would sit there and talk for hours just as they had done when Raven was growing up. When people would come to her for help, they did not even care that Key-Na had died. After half a spring of heartache Raven decided to move away from Rain Rock. Away from people who acted as if Key-Na meant nothing, even though Key-Na had saved some of their lives and the lives of several children. Raven wanted to move somewhere deeper in the forest where she could be happy, she hoped.

Raven told no one that she was leaving. She packed all that she would need the night that she decided to leave. She put her knife onto her belt along with an herb pouch. She grabbed her backpack and put her extra set cloths and her heavy winter boots. She also grabbed her sharpening stone; Key-Na always told her that a sharp knife is the best knife. The next day at mid-day, after no one had come, she grabbed what she had packed. As she took her cloak off the peg by the door she was struck with the memory of when Key-Na gave it to her. She closed her eyes to see the memory more clearly.

It was a very cold winter night, Key-Na pulled a wrapped package out from under her sleeping area and handed it to Raven. When Raven opened it there was a beautiful cloak. Key-Na always said that she had made it with magic so that Raven was always warm no matter what.

Before Raven walked out the door, she grabbed her two water skins and the one sentimental item that she had to have. It was Key-Na's necklace; she always wore it when she would help those who were sick or at birthing. Raven put the necklace on, walked outside and closed the door to the only home she had any memory of. Before she headed off on her adventure, she walked to Key-Na's grave to tell her goodbye.

"Key-Na I am leaving this area; it hurts too much to stay here and help the very people that don't even care that you are gone. I am planning on going deeper into the woods. With what you taught me; I am hoping that I will be able to find a new home where I can help people. I am planning on following the game trails. That way hopefully, I will be able to have plenty of food and water. I love you and I will miss being able to come and see you, but I have no choice." With her last words she placed a bouquet of flowers on the grave and walked away.

Raven had been walking through the woods for about a week, the weather had been pleasant during the day and warmish at night. The dense trees with their varying colors of green and golden gave her a sense of tranquility, something she desperately needed after her heartache. The tall pines and mighty oaks reminded her to be strong and endure. The aspen and willows reminded her of Key-Na. The way that she would be strong but had the ability to bend as well.

Even when the forest was extremely dense, she did not feel alone because she could hear the birds chirping or the squirrels in the trees chattering away. She would have talked to the animals, but she only heard birds and squirrels; she never saw any. She would see several different animal tracks but never the animal that made it.

As she walked, she gathered nuts and berries to eat along the way. She filled her water skins up every chance she got, it didn't matter if it was from a standing pool of water on the ground or in natural basin in a rock or tree stump.

In the evenings, if she was tired, she would crawl under a thick bush where the ground was softened by the dead leaves that had collected there. Or she would find a hollow tree in which to sleep where leaves and pine needles had collected. There were a couple nights that she continued walking well into the night. Not being concerned about seeing in the dark, she had always been able to see as brightly at night as she could at midday. Finally coming to a stop when she was too tired to go any further on those nights, she laid down by the path not caring what she slept on.

On the beginning the 12th day she noticed that the weather had turned cold, and the wind was bending the tops of the trees over and having enough force to reach through the canopy. She was almost blown off her feet on several different occasions. She knew that a huge storm had to be coming in and it would be best to find a safe dry secure place to spend the night.

She picked up her pace, in hopes of finding something before it began to rain. She had seen the large boulders in the distance between the trees; she headed towards them in hopes that she could find shelter in between them. As she came around, she saw that the boulders made a semi-circle around an outcropping. The way that the boulders stood the wind could not get to her and the outcropping proved a large enough area that she was protected from the rain. That was the worse night she had had in a very long time. With her being more interested in finding a safe place to wait out the weather she had not picked any berries along the way. She looked around for anything to eat in her shelter and found nothing. She wrapped her cloak closer around herself and leaned into the area under the outcropping finally falling asleep well after midnight, when the thunder and lightning had stopped, and the wind had calmed down.

The next morning, she awoke feeling a strong pull in the direction that she had been traveling in. her stomach growled and her throat felt almost raw from thirst, spurring her into action to go hunting for any rain that had collected and disappointingly, she could not find anything to eat or drink. She was very upset by this but continued to head in the direction that she was being pulled. Over the next two days she began to wonder if she would ever find where she was being pulled to. She also began to wonder if she would ever find anything to eat or drink again. As both water skins were empty.

It had been two days since she had last eaten or drank anything when a little after mid-day she stumbled into a meadow. As she looked around, she noticed that someone had planted fruit trees and roses as well as healing plants around the edges of the meadow. She heard the sweet sound of running water over rocks. She stumbled towards the sound and found a medium size brook with cool clear water. As she quenched her thirst, she looked around at the meadow again. She noticed the about 20 feet away from the brook was an oddly shaped hill. As she looked at the hill, the clouds moved away from the sun allowing sunlight to hit the ground. She saw a glint of more sunlight reflected on what could be a window.

It was hard to tell because; there were thorns, vines, as well as moss everywhere, covering everything. Raven walked around the hill and concluded that it was really a house or cottage of some type. She could tell that there was what could be two chimneys. Once she came back around to the window that had caught her attention, she pulled out her knife and began to cut the vines and thorns. She had such an over whelming urge to unbury the house, that she didn't notice that the thorns were slicing into her hands. It took 3 hours of cutting before she was able to really identify the building.

Raven was shocked at what she found under all the overgrowth; it was a medium size stone cottage. As she continued clearing off the overgrowth, she discovered that there were four windows in all. Each faced a different direction, north, south, east, and west. She also found on the east side of the cottage there was a weathered wooden door. She could only see in through the south facings window, all the other windows were covered by fabric from the inside.

Worried that she might be at someone's home she looked in the south facing window. She was amazed at what she saw, on the three walls that she could see there were shelves that went from the floor to the ceiling beams full of books and boxes. There was what looked to be a shelf bed built into the west wall. There were two fireplace the small one at the foot of the bed made from what looked to be brick and clay most likely a baking oven. Raven figured it was that way so that the person in bed could stay warm in the winter as the bread baked. The other was larger and up in the northeast corner. She could see a table as well as a work bench and there appeared to be a counter with a wash basin in the southeast corner.

She went around to the door, as she grabbed the leather latch on the door it broke in her hand but didn't allow the door to open. Determined to get in the house she pulled her knife and slid it between the door and the frame and began to pry the door open. She could hear the weathered wood creak in protest at the prying, but she continued her task. As soon as the door opened there was a gust of air that smelled horrid. Raven could tell by the smell that the house had been closed for many years and that something had gone bad.

She decided to let the house air out a bit and instead of going in she began to look more closely at the trees and plants to try and find something that she could eat. There were plum trees as well as apple trees Raven figured that these would be ripe in a couple of months. The cherry trees that she found had already bore their fruits and the birds or other animal had eaten all of them. She was able to find a large patch of blackberry and raspberry brambles that had enough ripe berries for her to eat something. There were all kinds of edible plants. Raven figured between the plants and berries she had about two weeks before she needed to find a town to buy supplies. She was worried about how to pay for them, but she decided to take things one thing at a time. By the time that she was done looking at all the plants and trees she was back where she started at the house.

As Raven walked into the house, she noticed that the shelves were full of all kinds of books and different size boxes and bottles. Even though the house had been closed for some time there was hardly any cobwebs or dust. Everything except the windows looked to be clean as if someone had just been there. Raven felt feelings of warmth, and welcome from the house. It felt the same as her home before Key-Na died. It was almost as if Raven's choice to leave Rain Rock, was a way to leave her loneliness and despair behind her and find happiness and peace in a new home.

Walking in Raven could see that under the water basin, there was a cupboard. Under the south window there were some low shelves. They looked to be the only open shelves in the whole house. She looked at the southwest corner and saw that it was had the tall shelves as well however it looked to be all books. She walked over to the southwest shelves and looked at the books. All the books looked to be on either plants or animals. However, as Raven looked at the other shelves, she found two that were not. One was titled Myths and Legends and the other was titled Maps. Raven was so happy to see the books; she had left all her books at Key-Na's house in Rain Rock not wanting to be weighted down. Key-Na had instilled in Raven a love of books. Raven pulled down one of the books on plants she opened it and began to cry. The book had been written in Key-Na's beautiful handwriting. As Raven looked further, she saw that there were drawings and those were done by Key-Na as well. Raven closed the book and held it to her chest. She could picture Key-Na bent over the table with a candle burning late into the night writing and drawing. Raven had seen her do it many nights as she had grown up.

Raven set the book down on the bare mattress and continued looking at all the books. She saw that each was done in Key-Na's handwriting. As she would finish a book, she would set it on the bed so that way she didn't grab the same book twice. The last book that Raven took down to look at was the Map book. The first map was what looked to be the general area; Raven continued to look at the others maps and deciding to come back to that map later. The maps after that dealt with the best places to find certain herbs and there even looked to be one about a cave system.

By the time she had finished looking at all the books and had placed them back on the shelves it was getting dark and chilly. With what time of day, it was, Raven decided to go out and look around the meadow for loose wood, at least enough to make a fire in the baking oven. To keep her warm as she slept. She was able to find quite a bit of wood at least enough to last her the night. After she got a fire going, she saw in the fire light that there was a box under the bed.

In the box Raven found 15 candles and a little bit of rope. Raven took the rope and ran it through where the leather had broken so she would have a handle on the outside of the door again. She went back inside and lite a candle once that was done, she started to take down the boxes from the shelves and look in them. After Raven looked in a box, she would set the box on the table (where she had set the candle) most were empty some held dried herbs and the contents of a couple of them had gone rancid.

Raven noticed that on the bottom inside of the last box there was a ribbon attached. When she pulled on the ribbon it pulled up the bottom of the box, she looked down and saw a small leather bag. As Raven pulled it out a there was a jiggling sound muck like that of coins hitting each other. She sat down on one of the three chairs at the table and poured the bag out. There were 100 pieces of gold and 50 pieces of silver that fell on to the floor including a piece of paper. She unfolded the paper and saw that it was a note.

To whom it concerns,

If you have found this than I hope that you are not a thief but someone in need of this money. The reason that I have left it is because it was given to me as blood money. A wealthy man wanted his wife and unborn child murdered. As a healer I could not do this in good conscience. So instead, I fled with the woman and her unborn child. I only hope that in doing this the woman and child are safe and not hunted after. I have turned my self over to the fact that I will never be able to come back to my home. The one saving grace in this is that I will be able to live with myself. I hereby turn all the possessions in this home and the knowledge that is here over to you to do with as you want. I truly hope that you are not a thief but a healer and will be able to find my knowledge helpful and my home inviting.

Sincerely
Key-Na

Raven was amazed that Key-Na had enough bravery to save the woman and had not lost her head in the process. She went over and picked up the book with the maps in it and looked more closely at the maps, she saw that there used to be a town about 12 miles away it was called Rose Hedge. She decided that the next day weather permitting, she was going to walk to town and see if it was still there. If it was, she would buy some supplies that she needed. Raven wrapped up in her cloak and settled onto the bed just before she fell asleep, she thought of Key-Na and sent a silent thanks to her for giving her another home.

That night Raven dreamed of Key-Na the first time she had since Key-Na passed away. Key-Na she was sitting at a table her snow-white hair was pulled into a braid that draped over her shoulder. She had on a dark red top, and she was reading a book. Raven walked over to her and sat across from her. Key-Na looked up closed the book and spoke

"I see you have found where some things began, and other things ended child of my heart. I understand why you left, and it was a good thing. Your life will be forever changed now from the path I thought to set you on. I am so proud of you, never forget who you are." Raven awoke briefly with tears in her eyes. The baking oven was still giving off heat. Raven staired at it for a bit as tears fell down her face. She quietly cried herself gently back to sleep.

Chapter 2

*T*he day dawned bright with the promise of warm weather and plenty of sun. Raven grabbed the pouch that had the money in it, she left 10 gold pieces and 10 silver pieces in the pouch. She then put the rest of the coins back in the bottom of the box; she tied the pouch on to her belt and hid the box under the mattress.

She started walking, she figured she could make it to town by mid-day. As she walked down the center of the road, she let her mind wonder. Thinking of all the walks that her and Key-Na had gone on while she grew up. She also wondered who it was that Key-Na had saved. If the child had lived and where it was.

It was close to mid-day when Raven realized that she was no longer walking by herself. She was being paced by a large, black horse, about five feet or so in the woods. Raven changed direction and slowly walked towards it. It stood there staring at her breathing hard its head hung low. She walked all the way around the horse and noticed three things. One that it was a gorgeous mare another was that there was a nasty wound on its right flank. The wound was oozing blood. The last thing was that the mare had a simple rope bridle. As Raven walked around the mare did not seem to shy away from her or appeared to be aggressive in anyway.

Raven took a closer look at the wound on the mare's flank it looked like it might have been from a bear or other large, clawed animal. Raven looked around for something that she could make into a bandage to help slow the bleeding. She saw a small cluster of ferns and there was a large patch of mud by the road. Not really seeing anything else around that she could use, she used the mud from by the road and ferns to make a patch for the mare's injury. Raven knew that it wouldn't heal the wound, but it would stop the oozing for a while.

The horse was a beautiful black Friesian mare and Raven knew that it had to belong to someone. Her mane was well combed, and her hide shinned like it had been brushed recently. Raven figured she would take the mare to town and see if anyone knew who she belonged to. She grabbed the rope halter and experimental started walking off towards the road, the mare followed without hesitation. It took another hour to reach town, by that time and the mare was limping not too badly but enough that Raven wanted her to rest she was also rather hungry. Raven asked an older man.

"Excuse me sir do you know where I can put this mare so that it can rest and get some feed? Also is there somewhere nearby that I can get something to eat?"

The old man looked as if he had seen a ghost. He turned as white as his hair and without another word or even a look he turned and ran towards the middle of town. Raven along with the mare not knowing what else to do, followed slowly behind the gentleman. Raven figured that he was letting someone know to expect them. As she walked, she was able to look around and she noticed that the homes looked to be very well taken care of. Also, the streets were stone instead of dirt unlike in Rain Rock.

It must have been market day, because the street was lined with carts selling all kinds of things. From wonderfully spicy smelling meat pies to beautiful exotic cloth. The mare stayed close behind Raven. Raven noticed that when people walked by her and the mare that they would stop and stare. At first Raven thought that it was due to the mare, however a young man dressed in what looked like high quality messenger's clothing came running up to them. He bent over at the waist to catch his breath before he spoke in a breathlessly voice.

"The lord of the town wants to see you." Raven was a bit worried because she was new to town and did not think that she had broken any laws. That was when she knew that everyone had been staring at her instead of the mare. Not wanting to be in any more trouble than she guessed she already was in, she followed him leading the mare with the rope. Raven and the mare walked behind the young man up the only hill in town. To a very large wall that looked to be around a very large home of some type.

Raven noticed as she walked under the great iron portcullis that it had very nasty spikes on the end of each bar. Once she was pass the gate Raven could see that what she thought was a large home was in fact a keep set on the top of a cliff. She could smell the ocean and hear the surf it was nothing like what she had ever experienced before. She felt very small and insignificant. She heard the flapping of fabric in the wind and looked up to see a blood red flag with a gold symbol upon it flying from the tallest tower.

As a way for her calm her nerves she began studying the workmanship of the keep. It was hard to see through all the white roses and ivy climbing up the walls. For what she could see the work was very finely done. The blueish grey stones seemed to fit together as if by magic. The windows looked to be large enough to allow plenty of sun light in during the day. Raven was surprised to see brightly the windows shined in the sunlight.

"Who lives here?" Raven asked the young man.

Without stopping he responded

"The Lord of this territory, who has been looking for you for a very long time."

Raven began to worry even more because she knew that she had never been out of Rain Rock before in her life. Before Raven could ask any more questions they were at the front door of the keep. The young man banged on the dark wooden doors 3 times and then waited to be let in. When the door opened Raven could see that the inside was as gorgeous as the outside. The windows letting all the sunlight in made the floor almost a blinding white with hints of pink. The young man turned around and motioned for Raven to follow. When Raven went to walk into the house the mare grabbed the back of her cloak with her teeth and pulled her back.

As Raven turned to reprimand her when she noticed that the mare was shaking. The mare's eyes were wide, and her ears were laid back against her head. Because of the way that Raven was raised she took heed of the distressed that the mare was showing fright decided that they would leave. Raven looked quickly around and did not see anyone close enough to stop her. She grabbed the mare's mane while keeping ahold of the rope and swung herself up on to the mare's back. The mare reared up and spun on her back hooves once she was facing the way they had just came. The mare took off like a lightning bolt out the gate and continued running out of town. The mare did not stop until they were almost halfway back to the meadow.

The mare had slowed to a walk by the time they were at the meadow, her sides were heaving, and her wound had opened, and she was limping very badly. As Raven slid off the mare's back her legs gave out and she collapsed on the ground. She had never ridden that long or that hard before. Her bottom hurt a little and for the first time in her life, she was glad that she had a little bit of extra padding.

Key-Na used to tell Raven that her having womanly curves was a good thing, Raven never believed her until now. The mare limped over to the brook and drank her fill. Then she came back over to nuzzle Raven. While the mare was at the water Raven noticed how the sunlight played over the mare's skin and muscles. The coloring that it produced reminded her of the obsidian stones that used to cover the ground outside of Rain Rock. With the mare nuzzling her Raven asked, "How does the name Obsidian sound?" The mare nickered and bumped Raven a little. Which she took as a sign that the mare liked the name.

Raven shakily stood up and waited a minute to be sure that her legs would hold her and then walked into the house. Once inside she grabbed the bucket from by the wash basin along with a scrap of cloth that she had found in with a bunch of others in one of the boxes. As Raven walked back out of the house and over to the brook, she asked out loud.

"What was that all about?" Raven filled the bucket up and then walked over to Obsidian.

Raven washed the remaining mud and fern mixture from Obsidian's flank. As she was washing the wound, she realized that she was correct in thinking that a large claw had made the cut. Raven dumped what water she had not used in the cleaning and went over and filled the bucket up again. She swished the water around in the bucket to rinse the blood, plant, and mud out, she then dumped the dirty water.

With the bucket filled with clean water once more Raven went inside to focus on getting a fire going. She poured the water into one of the three pots that she had found under the counter, and then walked back outside to see what all healing plants she could use for Obsidian. Raven saw that there was a bayberry bush on the west side of the meadow and chamomile grew along the brook.

After gathering those two ingredients she went inside and put one of the pots over the fire. She then added the plants and just enough water to cover them and brought that all up to a boil. Her plan for forming all of it into a poultice took a bit of time but it did work. When it was done, she took it outside and because of the gumminess from the berries she was able to create a patch that stuck to Obsidian's flank rather easily. She stayed away from town for a bit, she could not think of why the Lord had wanted to see her.

To stay safe, she spent the next few days gathering herbs to dry and reading books. She focused mostly on the plant books so that she would be able to continue her trade with the herbs that were in the area. Raven also changed Obsidian's poultice often. She was very happy at how well the gash was healing.

Chapter 3

Raven stayed away from town as long as she could, but her food was running low, and she needed some other clothes. Raven left Obsidian at the meadow so she would not draw any extra attention to herself. Also, as a way not to draw any attention she tied her long-stripped hair into a braid and tucked it under her hood so that way people would be less likely to see it. She went outside by the brook and grabbed some mud and smeared it on the cloak to make it look like she had been out in the woods or out working in a field. She knew that she couldn't do anything about her unique eyes except keep her head down and not look at anyone for a long time. Raven made it to town without any incidents. Once in town while keeping her head down she asked a merchant where she might find the general store. She was directed to head to the center of town. It was a large building very hard to miss. Raven thanked the person and kept her head down as she walked away. The merchant had been correct it was very hard to miss the bright blue colored building.

She walked into the store keeping her face hidden. It was rather easy in the dimly lit store. She waited for the other customers to leave before she approached the counter. The man behind the counter had his back to her. She studied him, he was little overweight but not portly, he had dull red hair and from what she had heard he had a pleasant voice.

"Excuse me sir. I would like to buy some supplies." Raven tried to make her voice sound far more confident than she felt. She was so afraid that someone would see her and call the guards.

"Of course, young lady how can I help you?"

"I need some flour, honey, enough root vegetables and dried meat to last my family a month. Some clothes for my sister and brother along with a couple of extra blankets. A good lamp with oil, some candles, soap powder and lastly some rope." She kept her head down so she was not sure what he was thinking.

"Wow that is a lot of things young lady. I hope you have a cart."

"No sir I unfortunately do not. Can you recommend some place?"

"Well, you can go down to below the keep before you get to the docks you will come across the livestock pens. There you can get a cart and livestock for a fair price."

"Thank you very much sire I hope this is enough. I will be back shortly for the supplies" she said as she laid 3 gold coins down on the counter. Before she could blink, he had the coins off the counter and in his pocket. She made her way to the base of the cliff keeping her head down. She knew when she was at the livestock pens by the smell and the sounds.

Raven watchfully made her way to the base of the cliff and the stock yards there. Looking up she could see the back of the keep. The ivy and roses barely crept around to the back. The bluish grey stones looked very weathered and worn were they overlooked the ocean. She was so mesmerized by the sight that she walked into a person knocking her hood back and causing her to fall on her butt.

"Let me help you up miss." Said a skinny old man as he reached his gnarled hand towards her.

"Thank you, sir I am so sorry for, not watching where I was going." She said as she reached her hand out to him. Once she was standing, she quickly covered her hair.

"So, miss how can I help you today?" He asked, Raven was very aware that he was studying her very closely.

"I need a large cart, as well as an animal to pull it. I believe we need a cow as well as 3 or 5 chickens and feed for all of them."

"Okay well for all of that including a mule to pull the cart it will be 20 silvers. You will have to pick the feed up at the general store I don't keep it down here." He said as he looked at what she wanted and did the sum of all in his head.

"My Father only gave me 10 silver pieces however I do have this." She said as she handed him 2 gold pieces. As soon as he had the gold coins in his hand he smiled, and the gold disappeared into a pocket as if it was never there. Raven got the impression that gold was rare here just as it was in Rain Rock. As the man put the gold into his pocket, he called a young man over to help Raven hook up the donkey to the cart.

He looked close to Raven's age with his long black hair tied back away from his face with a piece of leather. He was taller than her by about six inches putting him at about 5 foot 10 inches. She could see that his eyes were hazel and seemed to have a twinkle about them, making her think that he was quick to laugh. The young man loaded the chickens in a crate and tied the cow to the back of the cart. Only then did he hook the mule to the front of the wagon not knowing what to do Raven stood off to the side a watched intently. As she watched the young man, she got a feeling of comfort and protection from him. Positive that she had imagined it she ignored the feelings.

"So do you have feed for the animals?" the young man asked his voice reminded Raven of a soft breeze on a hot summer day.

"Not yet. The gentleman that sold me the animals said I had to go up to the general store to pick int up. I have to go back to the store anyway and pick up the rest of my supplies so I will get some feed then."

"Well, no offence but you don't look all that strong so I will come with you to help you load the feed bags. They tend to weight a bit." He said the last part with a chuckle.

As Raven climbed up on to the cart bench she snapped the reins, to get the mule going. The young man fell in to walking beside the cart as they headed back to the general store. Once at the store the young man told her to stay with the cart and he would get everything that had been bought and the feed as well. It was not long before the man was loading up Raven's supplies and the feed sacks as well. Raven watched him noticing how very handsome he was, and even though he did not look to have much for muscles he moved the heavy feed sacks as if they weighted nothing. With his black shoulder length hair pulled back from his face. He was the most handsome man she had seen before. Once he was done Raven thanked him and headed home.

"Thank you for your help. I can manage from here. I hope to see you again." with that parting word she snapped the reins and got the mule walking back to the meadow.

Raven noticed as she was heading home that there were a lot of soldiers on the road, they looked to be heading into town. Not wanting to draw any attention herself she hunched over more and tried to look as insignificant as possible. By the time that Raven got back to the meadow she was sore from having to bend over so much on the way home.

As well as being bent over she had been fighting with the mule for control as to where they were heading the whole way home. The mule had wanted to graze along the way. All Raven wanted to do when she got home was get off the cart and go to bed. She knew that she had to unload the feed and chickens along with unhooking the mule and untied the cow. She grabbed the rope out of the box and tied the cow to a close tree on the other side of the brook down from the house so she could continue to have clean water. She then went back to unload the feed bags.

Raven was shocked at how heavy the feed bags really were. She barely managed to prop the bags against the house before she wanted to collapse from the strain of moving them. She knew she still had to unload her supplies from the cart. She mustered her strength again. She went back to cart and forcefully moved it over to the feed bags to protect them from any rain that might fall. Knowing that she was almost done she pushed off her fatigue and unloaded her supplies. As she was unloading, she discovered that there was an extra box in it was more flour some eggs and more honey and a loaf of bread that smelled sweet.

She was very tired, but she knew she had to secure the animals for the night. She placed the chickens close to the house and used her knife to open one of the feed bags a little, she reached into the bag and gave chickens a little bit of the feed. The mule had wandered off to where Obsidian was grazing so Raven didn't worry about feeding it. After she decided that all the animals would alright for the night she went inside. She got afire going in the main fireplace and then took her bucket out to the brook so she could get some dinner started for herself.

She put a bit of water into a cook pot leaving the rest in her bucket. she then cut up a bit of smoked meat, a small carrot, and a small potato. She let it slowly warm up over the fire once the potato was soft, she pulled it off and spooned some of her humble stew into a bowl. As she ate her dinner, she cut a piece of the sweet bread for a treat and realized that it had dried apples in it. She made a mental note to thank the store owner for the treat when she was next in town.

After she was done eating, she warmed up the rest of the water once it was very hot, she poured it into the wash basin and washed her dishes. After the dishes were washed, she took the basin out and dumped it away from the house and brook. She put it away and grabbed her bucket once more filling it with water from the brook and placed it again by the fire. As the water warmed up, she unfolded two of her new blankets and placed them on the bed. She then striped out of her traveling cloths unbraided her hair and washed off briefly. By the time she was clean and dry she was almost dropping from exhaustion. Not even caring that she was naked she crawled into bed. Her last thought for the night was that she was going to have to back into town the next day.

Chapter 4

Raven awoke the following morning with a clear idea of what needed to be done once she reached town. First thing was she was going to have to buy some lumber, the second was that she was going to have to hire someone to build or to teacher her how to build a shelter for the animals.

She got up off the bed went to the table and cut off some more bread to break her fast. She then grabbed out the boy clothes hoping that the person in charge of the lumbermill would be more willing to deal with a boy as opposed to a young lady. To help her with the illusion of being a boy she braided her hair again and this time stuck it down the back of her shirt. She grabbed the bucket and went out to milk the cow it was a bit harder than she thought but after a couple of false starts she was able to get a full bucket of milk. She put it in the house under the water basin in hopes of keeping it cool. She put her new cloak on and realized that it was bulkier than her old one and very none descript. She noticed that when she pulled the hood up all the way that it fell into her face a little bit. She hoped that it would help the illusion even more.

She headed out the door again after grabbing the money pouch to go hook up the mule to the cart. It took almost an hour of chasing the mule around the meadow before she finally got it hooked up. She was rather annoyed as she headed into town. This time with her head up and the hood of the cloak pulled down.

Raven started the trip in high spirts even though she was annoyed at the mule until she saw a group of soldiers surround a young girl. She stopped the cart not knowing what else to do.

"Who are you and where are you going?" One of the soldiers said to the young lady in a very gruff voice.

"My name is Serina, I am a maid at the inn in town. How may I help you?"

"Have you any proof you are who you say you are?" He asked still very gruff.

"You can ask my employer Matthew he owns the inn. Now I must go or else I will be late for work." Serina said as Raven watched her try and push past the soldiers. Before Raven could do anything one of the soldiers turned grabbed the mule's bridle and asked Raven.

"Who are you I don't think I have seen you before." Raven sat terrified on the cart. The soldier asked again who Raven was. Before Raven could come up with a lie the girl Serina came to her rescue

"He is my cousin; you must forgive him he does not speak born that way I am afraid. Tommy how nice of you to bring the cart and come with me into town. If you gentlemen are done accosting me, I need to get to work." She said rather sarcastically and waited for the soldiers to decide what they were going to do.

"Very well you may leave but I will be talking to Matthew and verifying that you are who you say you are." The gruff voiced on said as he stepped to the side, the others followed his lead. Serina smiled at Raven and offered her hand as if asking for a hand up. Raven obliged and helped her onto the cart bench and slid over so Serina had enough room to sit. She got the mule walking again and after being down the road a bit Serina said.

"If you are going to act like a boy you need to practice more. Just be glad that it was soldiers out looking and not the Lord or his son. Either one of them would have seen right through you. Hunch over more in your cloak and hide your hands, keeping your hood up helps. So where are you going?"

"Is that how you knew that I was a girl?" Raven asked in a stunned voice but did not stop the cart.

"Yes, with where I work you learn to see deeper than the soldiers are thought to. I saw you face from my angle as well as your hands. The soldiers are being told to look for any young women on their own. I guess the young lord lost one of his playthings or something. I truly have no idea but if you want to be seen as a boy then heed my warnings. Also, when you talk put your chin into your chest it will deepen your voice."

"I will heed your warning as for where I am going, I was heading to the lumber mill, and I was hoping to hire someone to build an animal shelter or at least teach me how to build one. Where would you like me to drop you off?" Raven asked testing out Serina's suggestion. Much to Raven's surprise it worked she sounded more like a young man to her own ears anyway. Serina laughed.

"Well at least you don't sound like a girl anymore, but I would say keep the talking to a minimum. You can drop me off by the center of town."

When Serina and Raven got just to the edge of the center of town they stopped. Serina jumped down and said.

"Stay out of trouble Tommy and remember what I said." And she waved over her shoulder at Raven as she walked towards what looked to be a large two-story building. Raven heard a loud shout from the far end. She jumped down and began walking over that direction. She saw there were about 20 or more young girls in the center of town they all had long black hair.

Worried that she was the cause she turned around and headed back to her wagon as unhurriedly as possible when all she wanted to do was run. When she got to the cart, she realized that she had forgotten to ask Serina where the lumber mill was. She saw a man standing with his back to her next to her cart she tapped him on the shoulder. Remembering at the last minute to drop her chin she asked

"Can you help me I am new and need the lumber mill." He turned and she recognized him. It was the young man from the stockyard that had helped her the day before. His hazel eyes got a look of pure shock when he saw her dressed as a boy. He bent his head down slightly and quietly asked.

"What are you doing dressed like a boy?" he hissed quietly as he grabbed her arm and try to shove her up on to the cart.

"I came to town to hire someone to help me at my home and to buy some lumber to build an animal shed for my livestock." Raven responded just as quietly no longer worrying about trying to change her voice as she climbed up on to the cart's bench

"Well, you can hire me I need out of town for a bit anyway" he said as he climbed up after her. He grabbed the reins and turned the cart around, so they were heading back out of town. Once there he steered the cart off on to a barely visible trail. It took another hour before they arrived at the mill. Once there he jumped down and went over to talk to a bear of a man. He looked as if he could pull up a tree with his own two hands. He towered over the other man by at least 2 feet. Raven was too far away to hear what was said but her new hired hand came over with a triumphant look on his face.

"So, Borris is going to cut us a deal. All the lumber we need along with the supplies for 20 silver pieces."

"I can give him 2 gold pieces would that be alright?" Raven asked silently hoping that it would be fine.

"What! You have gold? No wonder the James went running to the keep as soon as you left yesterday. Give me the gold I trust Borris he will be very happy with the 2 gold." He said as he held out his hand. She handed him the money and watched as he quickly headed back over to the person named Borris.

The wood and supplies were loaded up quickly. When it was done Raven expected her hired hand to come up front, but he jumped into the back and sat looking over his shoulder expectantly. She guessed that he was waiting for her to start moving. She turned the cart around and headed back to the main road. Making sure that she hunched over like Serina had said and made sure to hide her hands in her cloak. She kept a bit better control over the mule than the day before and made it back to the meadow without causing suspicion.

When they arrived back at the meadow Raven got down and noticed that someone had been there, there were large boot prints all over. All the animals were there except, Obsidian who was nowhere to be found. She walked around looking at the prints to try and determine if Obsidian had been taken or not. When Raven was about halfway around the meadow, she heard the young man call out.

"I found a horse, but I think it is hurt really badly."

Raven ran to where he was standing; and saw that Obsidian was on her side and she had large gash. This time it was on her ribs going up and down to where Raven could see the rib bones. Obsidian was breathing very rapid and shallowly, Raven could see blood bubbles pop up between the ribs. Raven was so upset that she fell next to Obsidian and began to cry.

"Help me get her on her feet and over by the house I may be able to help her survive. But we have to work fast" Raven heard the man say

Raven did not have the heart to argue with him she figured if he could save Obsidian's life, she would do all in her power to help him. Raven stood up and began trying to get Obsidian on to her feet. It took a lot of pushing and prodding as well as talking and finally begging her to get up before Obsidian did. Raven held her around the neck as they walked so that it would be harder for her to lie back down. Once they got by the house the man placed his hands on Obsidian's side and close his eyes. Raven let go of Obsidian's neck to see what he was doing. Both wounds began to close the one on her flank closed first then the one on her side. Raven was mesmerized watching the muscles and veins one by one grow over the bones and mesh together on her horrid side wound. By the time it was done it looked as if there had never been any damage, the skin had grown back then the beautiful black hair grew over the skin not even leaving a scar.

Raven was so mesmerized by what was happening she didn't even know the young man had fallen until she heard him hit the ground. She bent down afraid that he had given his life for Obsidian. When she felt a strong pulse in his neck, she felt a huge wave of relief. Realizing that he was just passed out from exhaustion she grabbed his arms in hopes of moving him in the house. She pulled with all her might, but he was just too heavy.

Not knowing when he would wake up, she decided that she would camp outside for the night so she could keep an eye on him. She gathered enough wood to have a fire for the night. When she had the fire burning to where she knew it wouldn't go out right away. She feed the animals looked over Obsidian again just to make sure that she was really healed. After being inspected Obsidian wandered away. Raven unhitch the mule from the cart and watched as is wondered off to join the horse.

As Raven sat staring at him, she unbraided her hair. She noticed that by fire light the young man looked younger than he seemed. She left him long enough to gather some food from the house for herself and him when he woke up. Remembering to grab the bucket of milk she was pleasantly surprised that it was still cool. She grabbed the bread some smoked meat and a cup she had found she headed back outside.

When the sun set, she ate her part of what she had grabbed for her supper. It was well after night fall close to midnight before he awoke. Raven was awake not wanting to sleep for fear of something happening to him. As he opened his eyes a single wolf howled mournful.

"How are you feeling?" Raven asked her voice full of concern

"My head hurts but I think I will live." He said, his voice not super steady but not sounding groggy.

"Great than you can explain to me how you were able to do what you did for Obsidian."

Just as he was about to answer the wolf howled again this time closer and very angry sounding. Raven was about to ask the young man if he knew how to keep wolves away. When a large gray blur raced towards the fire in direct line with her, it jumped the fire and crash both of its large front paws into her chest knocking her backwards. It pined her with it legs and full barrel chest sinking its large sharp teeth in to her right shoulder. Raven was so surprised that she didn't have a chance to scream and with the wolf's weight on her she couldn't get enough air to try and scream.

Raven was on the edge of hysterics when suddenly the beast was off of her, and she heard it running into the woods. However right before the wolf let go of her, she could have sworn that she that there was another animal growling. Raven was losing consciousness fast all she could think of was stopping the bleeding and clean the wound her last though before the blackness consumed her was that she wished Key-Na was there.

Chapter 5

aven awoke to hearing people arguing she knew it was the next day as she stared at her brightly lit cottage ceiling. She looked around and not seeing anyone realized that they were arguing outside very loudly.

"She is not here I am just her hired help"

"She is a wanted criminal, and you will surrender her by order of your noble lord!"

"I do not believe you. What proof do you have against her?"

"That black mare that was here a week ago she belongs to your lord!"

"He is no Lord of mine I am just a hired hand passing through. As for the horse as you see it is not here perhaps it was just wondering through as well."

"She was seen in its company when she first arrived therefore, she stole it now let us see her!"

"I am sorry to say that she left a couple of days ago and has not been back."

"Then you will not mind if we check the house?"

"Once again, I apologize when she left, she locked the door somehow and did not tell me how to unlock it. I believe that she did this to encourage me to get the animal housing done so I would have a place to stay, out of the weather." Raven was surprised at how calm and protective he sounded even though the guards were yelling at him.

"Very well I will take you at your word that she is not here, but I promise you that if we come back and she is here then you and her will pay the price for being criminals."

Raven did not hear anything for some time after that, so she decided to go back to sleep. When she awoke again it was to find herself covered in sweat and she was sitting bolt upright. Raven was not sure why she had awoken and then she heard a wolf howling it sounded very close by. Upon hearing the howl Raven made a strangled scream. She heard movement and then saw the young man had come over and sat on the bed beside her. He gently pushed her back down, so she was laying again.

"Shush do not worry the animals are sheltered and the doors to both their home and yours are bolted shut. Do you think that you could eat some soup and some flat bread?" Raven noticed that his voice had a note of concern in it.

"I would rather have water at the moment." Raven said faintly her throat felt raw and sore.

"Yeah, I should have offered that to you first, you have been sick for about a little over a week with a fever." He said sheepishly

He walked over to the water basin and filled a goblet for her. After handing it to Raven he walked over to the fireplace. Raven sat back up feeling very weak and drank the water. However, after a few sips even that became too much, and she laid back down and went back to sleep. When she next awoke, she saw that there was sunlight streaming in through the uncovered windows and the man was nowhere around.

Raven swung her legs off the bed and tried to stand but she was so weak that she fell back onto the bed. As she fell, she let out a little squawk sound. The man must have been right outside the door because he came bursting in and the bucket of water that he was carrying splashed onto him. Even though Raven was weak and sore she giggled a little bit before she could stop herself.

"I heard you make a sound I thought that something had happened." He said a little frazzled

"No, just trying to stand up but I have not had enough food of late. I should have died, how is it that I am not dead?" Raven asked. She moved the collar of her shirt and looked at her shoulder.

"My shoulder is healed quite a bit which tells me that I have been out of it for at least 10 or 15 days."

"10 Days actually and I have been feeding you broth when I could get you to swallow it." He said in a shy voice

He came over with the bucket of water and a cup and sat down; he filled the cup and handed it to her. As she tried to drink it her hands were shaking so bad that she could not hold it still. With a small grin he cupped Raven's hands and helped her drink the water. As he was holding her hands Raven began to feel an odd tingling in her hands as if she was holding bees in her hands instead of a cup of water.

When she was done drinking, he stood up and went to the small oven and pulled out a loaf of bread that had been set on the edge to keep warm. He handed it to Raven and then went over to the large fireplace a ladled out some thick stew into a bowl. He brought the bowl over and sat on the bed. Raven was excepting him to hand her the bowl when he handed her the spoon instead and held the bowl so that way it did not spill. He didn't seem to mind how long it took her to eat he just sat there looking at her. The flavor of the soup was amazing, she set the spoon in the bowl and tried to break off a piece of bread and failed. He set the bowl down and gently took the bread from her broke it and handed it back to her. Not saying anything at all after breaking the bread he picked up the bowl again and held it for her. It took a bit of time, but she ate all of the stew and all of the bread.

"Wow you can cook I am impressed. What did you use for that bread it was sweet and yet there was not any fruit in it? The stew was good too and did not taste like you used any smoked meat." She said after she had eaten everything.

"The bread was an old family recipe and I used some of your honey mixed with some of the dried lavender that you had gathered. Before you say anything, I did replace it with fresh lavender, and it is hanging in the rafters right now. The stew was made with fresh meat. I caught a rabbit this morning over by the berries; I thought that it would make a great stew."

"Okay now that I have eaten, please tell me your name I feel bad that I keep thinking of you as the man." He laughed a little bit, the sound made her feel good all the way from her head to her toes.

"My name is Azure. I am 25 winters old. My mother always enjoyed making bread when I was younger, and my father always enjoyed trapping hunting. Now pretty lady what is your name and why are the high Lord's guards after you?"

"My name is Raven. I am 19 winters old. My mother really did not seem to want to spend time with me. I have no idea who my father was he died before I was born. Once the healing woman Key-Na took me under her wing, my mother stayed away from me all the time. Key-Na seemed to enjoy me being around and even thought me how to heal others. She became more my mother than the woman that bore me" Raven spoke the last part with a sadness in her voice Even after all these years it still hurt that her mother didn't want her.

"You were raised by Key-Na! The woman who defined the high Lord and allowed his wife and unborn child to live and then left with them to keep them safe. That Key-Na raised you?" he asked me wide eyed and sounding a little in awe.

"I do not know much of her past. I just learned about her defying a noble man I am guessing that would be the high lord. She died at the beginning of winter I left the only home that I ever knew because I could not stand to stay there without her. The only thing I still have of hers is her charm necklace."

He asked very nicely to see it; Raven told him that it was in the blue box on the shelf in between the baking oven and the fireplace. As he pulled it down Raven caught a glimpse of a blade at the small of his back. It had a very ornate looking handle that looked to be made of silver or very polished white wood. He took the necklace carefully out of the box as if he was afraid that it was a snake or something else poisonous.

"This is her necklace alright she never took it off. I remembered the first time that I saw it I had just broken my arm falling out of a cherry tree. My mother brought me here and the necklace gave off a soft green glow as she took care of binding the arm and telling me what I had to do to help it heal."

He sat down on the floor holding it as if it were made of glass as he was sitting there, he began to quietly cry as if he was reunited with an old friend. Raven had the feeling that she should give him some privacy, so she laid down and rolled away from him and went to sleep. She was not sure how long he sat there and cried; she fell asleep to his soft crying sound. Raven slept until the next morning she awoke to see the sky through the window it was still slightly dark as if just before dawn.

Raven slowly and shakily made her way to the door and stepped out just in time to see Azure slip off into the trees. She grabbed a small loaf of bread off the counter and made her way back to the bed. Before she sat down, she grabbed the book on myths and legends from the shelf. Raven got so lost in the stories that time passed her by. She was so absorbed that she did not even hear Azure come into the house. When he placed his hand on her shoulder she screamed from surprise.

"Easy, easy, it is just me." Raven could tell by his voice that he was trying not to laugh at her.

"Sorry I got lost in the stories the bread is good again by the way. What did you catch today, and what is for dinner?" he looked confused until she told him that she saw him leave around dawn.

"I went to check one of my snares and found that whatever was in it was eaten by another animal before I could get to it." Raven was surprised to hear the pain in his voice at the fact that he allowed an animal that was defenseless in his trap be killed by another animal.

"However, I was able to catch some fish instead." He quickly said as he held up three large fish.

"Fish, I did not think that there were any fish in the brook."

"There aren't any I made a fish trap in the area coming from the river into the meadow. So that way when I lose the small game, I can still have some meat to bring home to you." he said with a half-smile he walked over to the water basin and cleaned the fish. Raven started to read the stories again; she figured that he would let her know if she could help. That night after dinner Azure unfolded a pallet and set it in front of the door.

"Where did you get everything for your bed?" Raven asked curiously.

"I found a large patch of high grass and I figured that you weren't using all your blankets so I would barrow a couple. I hope that it okay."

"It is fine I bought more than I needed anyway."

Their lives fell into a routine after that. He would leave every morning at dawn and come back in time to make dinner. Raven would milk the cow each morning and feed the chickens. He taught Raven how to make his mother's bread so she would have something to do during the day, other than just the morning chores. After dinner each night Azure would have her read out of the myths and legends book. He continued to place his pallet in front of the door at night. It helped to make her feel safer.

Raven's shoulder continued to heal extremely well it was still sore, however she noticed that she was becoming extremely restless, and her hearing seemed to be becoming more acute. One night a couple of weeks after the attack Azure was able to catch a couple of quail and the two of them roasted the quail up with a medley of root vegetables. Azure said.

"I have to go into town tomorrow for supplies do you need anything?" he asked as he laid his pallet on the floor.

"Something new to read and some paper so that way I can start to figure out the money usage and how much I owe you for all the work that you have done would be nice."

The next morning Raven stood in the doorway and watched him leave with the mule and the cart. Raven saw that Obsidian was off on the far side of the meadow. The cow had been milked and was eating a few green apples. The chickens were happily pecking at the ground as Raven gathered the eggs. She was getting very restless as the morning went on. So, she decided to walk around outside and check on the animals and the plants.

As she walked over towards the brook, she noticed that it sounded different than last time she had heard it. As she neared it, she saw that there was a pool that the brook feed into and then fed out of so that the pool never over flowed. Raven started to cry because she knew that Azure had created this wonderful thing for her. The water was crystal clear; she could see the stones on the bottom of the pool looked to be smooth. She stripped out of her cloths right then and there and stepped into the pool.

The water was cool but not cold and it felt so wonderful against her sore shoulder. The smooth rocks that lined the bottom of the pool told her that Azure really had wanted her to be comfortable in the pool. She leaned against the side of the pool and closed her eyes. Planning on just relaxing for a bit and then making some more bread.

She must have fallen asleep in the pool. She awoke with a start to the sound of branches braking. Raven looked around trying to see if she could see what had made the sound. The sun was high in the sky so there were really no shadows. She saw the trees that ran along the east side of the pool held some shadows but none dark enough to hide someone. She looked around meadow for what she could see of it.

Still not seeing anything so she tried to relax again but she could not shake the feeling of agitation and being watched. Raven climbed out of the pool grabbing her clothes and hurried towards the house. She heard a loud crash come from behind her as she looked over her shoulder, she saw five soldiers coming out from the woods. Before she could get inside, she was hit over the head.

Chapter 6

When Raven woke up, she could not see or hear anything which was very strange for her normally she could see in the dark very well. She was cold and it felt as if she was laying on a stone floor on her right side. Her ankles were tied together she pulled her knees up to her chest, and she noticed that her hands were tied behind her back with something that felt like rough rope. It did not feel like anything was on her face so wherever she was it was totally dark. It smelled like there was mildew close by, as well as sewage Raven was still naked so whoever had grabbed her from the meadow hadn't bothered to cover her before putting her in the dark. She began to shake so hard that her teeth were chattering she was not sure if it was from the cold or shock. She forced herself to go to sleep to try and escape the nightmare that she had awoke in.

When she opened her eyes again, she was still in the dark, but she was untied and there was something cold against her leg. She sat up and felt around for whatever it was and found that it was a metal bowl. She brushed her hand around the inside of the bowl and found what felt like a bit of bread and a small tin cup. She grabbed the bread and bit into it; it was old and stale and reminded her of how much she missed Azure's mother's bread after one bite she dropped the bread back into the bowl. As she began to cry at her dire situation.

Later after she calmed down, she grabbed the bread again and decided to eat it since there was nothing else. When she took a drink of water it had a brackish taste to it, but she knew that there was nothing else to drink and she had to keep her strength up. However, with all the movement her arm began to hurt and get stiff. She moved her hair enough to cover up her breasts and as much of her body as she could to try and retain some heat.

Raven forced herself to go to sleep sitting up to get away from the throbbing pain in her arm. It was a while later when she awoke to the sound of tapping, almost like boot heels hitting stone. The door opened blinding her she closed her eyes against the pain of the light as a metal bowl hit her feet, she was sitting with them in front of her. She heard a bolt slide and knew that the door was locked again. Once more it was stale bread and brackish water. She reminded herself that she had to keep up her strength she ate slowly.

Once she was done eating, she slowly stood up using the wall as a guide and a support. She leaned her right shoulder against the damp wall and started walking shuffling her feet as she walked so not to trip over anything. She stretched her left arm out in front of her as a way not to walk into a wall. She was able to take three shuffled steps before her hand on her left arm brushed against the wall in front of her. She kept her hand on the wall and continued to shuffle her feet until her toes were at the wall. Raven guessed that it was 4 feet or so from where she had been sitting.

Once she fully reached the wall, she repeated the process of leaning her shoulder against the wall and shuffling her feet. She figured that it was 8 feet to another wall. She continued along the new wall and found the wooden cell door 4 feet from the corner; the door was 3 feet across once she was on the other side of the door it was only a foot to the corner. She followed the wall again and just as she got to the corner her foot hit a bucket. Raven heard what sounded like fluids sloshed around in it and she noticed that the sewage smell was greater here. Raven jokingly thought *"great I get to pee in a bucket in the dark."* Raven worked her way back over to where she had been sitting and sat down. It was easy to find where she had been sitting because the stone floor was warmer than the rest.

Raven hurt so much from the cold floor and the fact that she still didn't have any of her cloths. She had no idea how much time had passed. Her hair helped some but not enough to stop her constant shivering. She was becoming depressed all she had to do during the day was walk around her cell, sit and when needed to walk over and pee in her bucket. She heard the tapping sound off and, on a lot, sometimes it would stop sometimes it wouldn't. When it would stop, the door would open blinding her and a bowl was slid in with a cup of water and bread.

Raven was being to question her sanity when the door swung open, and the room was filled with light. She waited with her eyes shut for the bowl to be slid in and hit her. Instead, she felt people grab arms and lift her up. She was so sore and stiff that the wrenching from the rough handling of her shoulder she ended up passing out from pain.

Once Raven became aware of her surroundings again there some type of rough cloth thrown over her. Her shoulder was throbbing and seemed to be on fire, and she was partially laying on her hair and partially lying on a hard floor. She also had a nasty headache. She could hear at least two men arguing in the same room as her. They seemed to be arguing about what to do with Raven.

"IF ANYONE EVER FOUND OUT THAT I HAD AN OLDER SISTER ONE THAT WAS NOT A BASTARD! MY FATHER WOULD BECOME THE LAUGHINGSTOCK OF THE TOWN AND ALL OF THE ROYAL CLANS!" The voice that was shouting sounded very male and very pissed off.

"Be calm sire it is possible that she is not of the Wolf-Tear's blood line. She might just look like she is part of it." Responded the other voice in a calmer but masculine voice.

"Please, she has the hair color the same slanted eye shape and according to the guards the same golden brown eye color. She looks a lot like that painting of that harlot that my father married. For those reasons alone she should be killed. Not to mention if she is who my father thinks she is I will lose everything I have tried so hard to make happen. She will receive everything I have worked for and not have to lift a finger to get it. NO Jerome!! She dies tonight after my father has had a chance to see her." the first man said in a quieter but disgusted voice.

Raven heard the door open and then slam-shut, she decided to act like she still was sleeping in case one of them was not gone. After a few minutes of silence, she slowly opened her eyes. Raven listened hard to make sure that no one was still in the room. When she didn't hear anyone, she slowly sat up and looked around. She was in a round room there was a wooden door and a few small arrow slit windows that had glass over them. The walls where a very dull gray unlike the blueish grey of the outside stones, there was a large tapestry hanging. The tapestry was very worn and damaged. There was no furniture in the room.

Raven noticed that someone had placed a burlap bag over her nakedness. As she stood it hit her about mid-thigh and it itched like she was sitting in a thistle bush. She stood up and walked 15 paces from one wall to the other. The wooden door had an inside lock and Raven was betting that there was locked on the outside of the door as well. Raven walked over and looked out one of the windows all she was able to see was water. It looked lovely with the blazing orange sun sinking down into the water. Raven watched it worrying about what would happen once it was down. She remembered that she had not seen any candles or a lamp in the room.

Once the sun was gone Raven sat in the middle of the floor facing the door. When she lost all the light, she heard a grinding sound from the locked door. She could clearly see around the room even without light. Not wanting to be at a larger disadvantage when the door opened, Raven stood up and made her way over to the wall. The door opened slowly; it seemed a person was slinking around the door almost as if they did not want anyone to see them. They closed the door quietly and then walked into the center of the room and asked quietly.

"Raven are you in here?" Raven recognized Azure's voice and went rushing and crying into his arms.

"I thought that I would die here and never see you again." She cried as his arms circled her waist.

Azure hugged her tightly and started to stroke her hair until she stopped crying. Once Raven was done crying, he handed her something that felt like a soft dress in her hands.

"I grabbed one of your dresses from the house and then stashed it in a hidey-hole, so I would have it handy when I found you. I am going to walk over to the other side of the room, so you can change into your dress." Raven watched him walk away from her and stop with his back to her; she quickly pulled off the burlap sack and put her dress on.

"I am ready" she said quietly.

"Okay, we need to go. I need you to be quiet, so we can get out of the keep and into town. From there we are going to a hiding spot. That way the soldiers won't find you." He said as he walked towards her.

They opened the door cautiously and looked up and down the hall to see if anyone was around. The hallway was dimly lit and appeared to be empty. They walked out hand in hand. After a few feet Azure pressed a stone in the wall, the wall moved, and a hidden stairway appeared. It was a dark stairwell and there were no torches on the wall that she could see. As if he knew what Raven was think Azure said confidently.

"Don't worry I can see in the dark enough for both of us."

"I can see in the dark as well." Raven responded defiantly.

As they stepped down two of the steps the wall slid shut behind them cloaking them in totally darkness. It was so dark that even though Raven knew that Azure was right next to her, she felt as if she was back in her cell. She began to panic until she felt Azure place his hand on her elbow. Raven placed her other hand on the wall and used it to keep her balance. It was slow going because she felt so weak. She almost fell a couple of times, the only reason she didn't was because Azure held her elbow in a vice like grip and prevented her from falling. Raven was so tired and scared; it felt like they had been in the secret stairway for hours.

Suddenly there were no more steps and the wall that Raven was using as a guide stopped against another wall. Azure griped her elbow harder to keep her from continuing to walk. Raven heard Azure mumble something and heard some cloth rustling as well as a grinding off to her left; suddenly the stairs were flooded in light. She was blinded and she felt Azure grab her around the waist and hug her to him as if to say that he was never letting go of her again.

"Just keep your face low and against my chest. Here is your cloak keep the hood up, it will hide your hair"

After she put her cloak on, she saw him lean down then he looped an arm under her legs and place his other arm across her back under her arms. He lifted her up as if she weighted nothing more than a child and nestled her up against his chest. Raven wound her arms around his neck and kept her face turned into his chest. Raven heard a few people ask Azure what he was doing. Azure always answered the same way. He would say

"This is my wife and servant, and she took a terrible fall. The reason that I am leaving the manor is to take her to the healer in the village."

Azure told anyone who tried to stop them that Raven had fallen, once they heard that they allowed Azure and Raven to pass without any problems. No one stopped them Raven was waiting to hear the sounds change from foot falls on the cobble streets to dirt. However, all she kept hearing was the ringing of Azure's boots on the stone. She heard a door open and close then he stopped moving, she moved her face away from Azure's chest and looked around. They were in a small room it contained a bed, a table, two chairs, and a small metal potbelly stove and on one wall there was a cloth hanging. Raven was betting that there was a window behind it. On the table there was a loaf of bread, some cheese and fruit. Azure bent down to allow her to place her feet on the floor. She turned her back to him and walked over to the chairs. Once there she could not keep her mouth shut any longer.

"How long has it been? How did you find me? Where are we? Who are you? How did you know about the secret hall? What did you say at before we left the stairway?" Raven's questions were flying out of her mouth. She noticed that they sounded a little hysteric, but after what she had been through, she felt that it was with in her rights to be a little hysteric.

Raven began to shake so bad that she could no longer stand. She grabbed one of the chairs, turned it around and slumped down into it before she fell on to the floor. Raven was so hungry that she grabbed the loaf of bread and tore an end off. As she ate, she saw that Azure had a curious look on his face, he opened his mouth several times as if to speak and then he closed it again. Finally, he seemed to work up enough courage and began to talk.

"First it has been almost a month since I last saw you. Second this is my place before I was staying with you. I stayed here for a few months. I figured that it would be a good place to work from while I was looking for you. When you vanished, I asked Hanson, from the general store, to keep an ear out for any odd news and then to let me know. That is the way that I found you. A couple of days after I talked to him two guards came into his shop and were bragging about how easy it was to capture the girl. Hanson knew that I was looking for odd news, so he let me know what was going on. I took on a job as a servant so that I could move around the keep without any problems. When I first found out where you were being held, you were in the dungeons. When I tried to get to you the first time, I was not sure if it was you, so I just opened the door and glanced briefly in as I slid the food dish in. When I was sure it was you, I decided that I would wait until I could get you out without anyone thinking anything about a missing prisoner. But by that time, I found out that you had been moved into the tower. I tried again to reach you, but I was told by a guard at the base of the stairs that you were to be left alone. Also, he informed me that the lord of the manor had taking interest in you. I asked the head kitchen master how I could get up to the tower without being seen. After being looked at rather skeptically I told him that I had an important assignment from the lord, which I was not to let anyone know of. He then nodded in an understanding way and told me about the secret stairway. I was giving thanks for finding you at the end of the stairway. The rest you know."

By the time he stopped talking he was sitting in the other chair, and he seemed rather calm. Raven's head was spinning with all the new information. She placed her head in her hands and tried to think about all that he had said. A month, how had she lost a full month, she remembered the soldiers coming to the pool and being hit over the head. Then wakening up in the dark and damp cell, she figured that was when she was in the dungeon. Raven thought that she had only been gone a few days but not a month. Feeling so overwhelmed she began to cry and start rocking back and forth in the chair. Raven heard Azure push the chair back as he stood up and placed his hands on her shoulders and began to rub it in slow circles.

"Let's get you over on to the bed, so you can get some sleep. I am afraid that when we leave here until we are somewhere safe you won't get much rest." he said in a depressed tone

"Well, where do you suggest we go that is safe?" Raven replied with a shaking voice as she looked up at him.

He scratched his head for a minute before grabbing her hand and helped her stand up. Raven did not even realize that she was still crying, until he cupped her face and brushed his thumb across her cheek. She saw him remove his hand and stick his thumb into his mouth to suck the tear off of it. Raven felt something in her shift and melt; she was so confused by her body's reaction that she stumbled slightly. Azure reached out and steadied her as he led her to the bed.

"Don't worry Raven I have already thought of a safe place for us to go. In fact, Key-Na gave me the idea. I saw her book of maps and having the extra time I studied them a bit while you were healing. I thought the caves would be the best and safest place. I figure that it would be close enough to get to in a day and it is honey combed enough for easy hiding." He gently pushed her down; she was sitting on the mattress as he finished talking.

When she sank down onto the feather mattress, she realized how very tired she was. As Raven laid down, she watched Azure walk over to the stove. She started to think how her life had changed in such a short time and it seemed as if it was not done changing. The last thing that she heard was wood being put into the stove. Raven felt as if she had only been asleep for a couple of minutes when she was violently shaken awake. She opened her eyes and started to panic thinking that she was back in the cell, because of how dark it was. Azure had gripped her shoulders and forcefully whispered

"Wake up."

Raven whispered. "What is going on?"

"Soldiers are going house to house looking for you. I doused the fire and I think if we stay quiet, we should be ok" just then there was a loud banging on the door, as the banging continued the doorknob was jiggled. Azure shoved Raven to the far side of the bed against the wall.

She fell off the bed even though she could have sworn that the bed was right up against the wall. Raven heard the bolt slide as Azure answered the door. Rather sleepy sounding he said

"Can I help you, captain?"

"We are looking for a woman that left the manor last night."

"Well as much as I wish I could help you there is no one here but me, much to my dismay."

"You were seen leaving this night with a woman that you claimed was your wife. However you say that you are here alone"

"I am sorry captain, but I have never been married however I do know that there are at least 4 other men at the manor that look much like me. Maybe one of them is who you are looking for."

"That may be however, we still have to come in and look around."

"That is fine. Please come in you can see everything in one glance." Azure said with confidence. Raven heard heavy boots walk into the room and then what sounded like someone striking flint and steel. There was a soft glow that she could see from see under the bed that filled the room with dim light from what she was sure was a candle.

"See captain no one here. Also, no place that someone could hide." Azure said

"Yes, I see that, well thank you for your time sorry to have awaken you I am sure the lord will expect to see you at the manor in the morning."

"I unfortunately will not be going back to the manor I was fired this evening over serving the lord the wrong meal. I served him bread and water instead of the roast squab and mashed turnips that he had requested. Due to that mistake, I was released from service rather forcefully without even being allowed my own supper. So now I will have to go back to my village and try and find work there much to my disgrace." Azure sounded very dejected at the last part. Raven didn't hear a reply, just heavy foot falls heading back out the door.

"You can come back out now. They are gone we but need to leave tomorrow at dawn."

"Why can't we leave right now?" Raven asked rather upset as she crawled up on to the bed and then off the other side to stand next to him by the table.

"Because if we leave right now, they will think that something is going on. We will leave tomorrow. We are going to have to find you some men's clothing so that you can slip out as a boy. I think Hanson has some clothes I will go over to the store now and hopefully Hanson will be awake it is almost dawn." He placed his hands on Raven's shoulders again and walked her backward until the backs of her legs hit the edge of the bed.

"You need to stay here and stay quiet. If anyone knocks on the door, I want you to hide in the same place that you did before. The door won't be able to be locked otherwise they will know that someone is here. I will be back as soon as I can." He said as he pushed her back down on the bed.

Just before Azure let go of her shoulders, he kissed her lips. Then turned and walked out the door. Raven was so shocked that she just sat there with her mouth open staring at the closed door. After the shock of the kiss passed, she tried to think of what to tell him when he came back. It was comforting that the candle was still burning so she did not have to think in the dark.

Several thoughts raced around in her head. Should she tell him that she didn't want to have feelings for anyone ever again? So that way she couldn't be hurt again, or should she tell him that she cares about him as well. Raven began to really think about if she cared about him, when someone began to pound on the door. The pounding became extremely persistent. Raven was sitting on the edge of the bed, so it was not hard for her to roll to the far side and slide between the bed and wall again.

It seemed like the knocking went on forever. Raven almost got up and answered the door just to make it stop. Then she would remember how the kiss made her feel and how if she answered the door, she would never feel it again. When Raven felt that she could handle no more, the door opened, and heavy footfalls marched across the floor in the direction of the stove and the foot of the bed. Raven held her breath fearing that if she breathed too loudly, she would be found. She silently cursed herself for leaving the candle burning on the table.

There was a loud squeal, like that of rusty hinges. Raven had to bite her lip to keep from screaming in fright. She heard flint being struck and then the popping of kindling and wood as the fire started. She was going crazy from not knowing what was going on, on the other side of the bed. Raven heard the person walk over to where she figured the table was. Someone pulled a chair out from under the table and then she heard the soft groan of wood as the person sat in it. There was a slight clink of metal as well. Raven's left shoulder and hip were starting to hurt from lying on the floor for so long she was however thankful that her chest was not very large, so she did not feel as if she was suffocating.

Raven thought that the person had gone to sleep because she had not heard any movement for a while. Suddenly she heard humming the voice was low like that of a man. She recognized the tune from a song that Key-Na would sing. It had been a few years since she had heard it, but it dealt with five brothers and wolves. Before she could focus on more of the song, she heard the door open, and a second person walk in.

"Captain, what can I do for you?!" Azure asked shocked and surprised tone "I am sorry that I was not home when you came, but I am glad that you let yourself in." Azure said in a much calmer and friendly tone.

"I am sorry but something about your story did not ring true. So, I figured that I would stop by unexpectedly just to do a double check your story. I have been here long enough to realize that there is no one else here otherwise they would have come out by now. So I will let you be. When are you planning on leaving for your village and is anyone going traveling with you?" the captain asked in a friendly tone as well.

"I am leaving tomorrow morning, and yes one of the grooms is going to travel with me. He is in charge of hunting for that black mare that went missing a couple of months ago. So, we are going to go to my village and maybe someone there has seen it, or at least that is the plan." Azure answered crisply. Just then Raven heard something be set on the table it sounded heavy.

"Very well, then I hope that you have a safe journey." The captain replied cheerfully.

Raven heard the chair be pushed back and footfalls heading towards the door. She heard the door open and close, then the loud ringing of the bolt slide home to lock the door and a heavy sigh.

"Raven, please tell me you are still here" Azure sounded breathless and scared as he asked that.

"I am here but I am stuck. Please help me I can't seem to move, and my arm feels like a piece of wood. My hip is not much better it has a dull ache. I really don't think that I can move without help." Raven said rather dishearten

The bed was pulled away from her so fast, she heard it crash into the table as she fell onto her chest. Her breath rushed out of her lungs from the impact, but it did feel good to be off of her arm and hip. She turned her head to the right and saw Azure kneeling down next to her, with a concerned look on his face. He bent over her back brushing her long hair away from her arm and began to tenderly rub her left arm. After a few minutes of him rubbing her arm, it started to tingle and hurt. Raven uttered a soft groan from the pain and Azure stopped immediately.

"Am I hurting you?" he asked anxiously

"No, not on purpose. I was just lying there for so long, that after you got the blood flowing it really hurt."

Raven pushed herself up into a sitting position and leaned her back against the wall. When she looked into his eyes, she saw that there was concern in them that melted her heart even more than the kiss they had shared. She reached out to touch his face, but he brought his hand up to catch hers instead. He threaded his fingers through hers and just sat there staring at her for a bit. As he stared into her eyes, she felt safe and not scared about what the future held.

Raven was not sure how long they sat there staring at each other. Azure broke contact first and cleared his throat. He stood up and walked to where the bed had been pushed to. He sat down on the bed and looked at her with a pained look.

"Do you know why the soldiers are looking so hard for you?" He asked softly

"I heard a couple of men talking while I was in the tower. One was positive that I was the lord's daughter. He was mad at that, something about him losing everything if I was the missing daughter. He then told someone named Jerome that I was to be killed after the lord saw me. But I don't understand how I could be who they are looking for. I was told that my father had died in a war before I was born. Also, if I was this person then Key-Na would have told me about it right." She said the last part in confusion.

"I am not sure why you would haven't been told these things, but you really are the lord's daughter. In fact, that was the reason that when you first came into town everyone was staring at you. Your mother looked like you but, she was taller. When she was here, she would walk through the town to check on her subjects. All of the royal families had homes here so that a court of the royal families could meet at anytime, to decide how best to help everyone under the clans rule."

"So, what happened? I found a letter from Key-Na stating that a wealthy man wanted his wife and unborn child murdered. If that was my father than why would he want me and my mother dead?" Raven was becoming more confused the longer that she listened.

"I am not sure; all I know is that he signed an agreement with one of the houses. Which stated any first-born child would be married to the first born of that family, as long as one was a boy, and one was a girl. I believe that your mother influenced that agreement. If you want my theory, your father wanted you dead even before he knew that you were a girl. He has always been selfish, and in marrying the clans together he would have had to share the power. Right now, the Wolf Tear clan is the strongest clan, so they are in charge for now. He probably figured that your mother would never stand for your death, so he wanted her dead as well. The man that would lose everything if the lord confirmed you as his child, is your half-brother. He survived his birth because his mother was a servant, and it was rumored that you had been born dead and that your mother died in childbirth. With both of you dead the agreement became void. There by absolving your father from any further agreements. The clans allow their leaders to marry once and only once." By the time he was done talking, Raven had stood up and had moved a chair for her to sit in over in front of Azure.

Raven sat down in the chair to think over everything. It was unsettling that her own father and brother wanted her dead. She couldn't seem to stay on one thought for very long; her thoughts were whirling around in her mind so fast that she started to feel nauseated. To calm her stomach, she forced herself to focus on things that she could do something about. She figured it would be best to learn about the other clans.

"Why are there not any other clans here anymore?"

"Your father ordered all of them removed from the city after your mother disappeared, he had the families believing that one of them had abducted her to prevent the union." Raven could hear the contempt in Azure's voice.

"So, what would have happened if I had married as it was arranged? Would things be better or worse? Who would I have married, and are they nice or mean?" Raven asked in a concerned voice. Azure chuckled softly from the bed where he was still sitting.

"So many questions well maybe to pass the time today I will tell you everything that I know. But first come here and see what all Hanson packed for us."

Raven got up and stiffly walked over to the table, there was a large sack on it. Azure stood up and dumped the sack out on the bed. Out tumbled a couple of changes of cloths in her size as well as a couple of larger size sets. There was a bottle of honey along with some bundles of herbs. There was another knife and some rope.

"I was not able to find your knife when I had to leave the cottage in a hurry. Before you worry Obsidian is fine, she is at the cave hiding. Unfortunately, something killed the chickens I think it was a. x. Good news is that Hanson said that he will take care of the cow and the cottage in exchange for the milk that he can get from the cow. The donkey ran off and I have not been able to find it anywhere. I think that the big wolf that attacked you killed the donkey." Azure said the last part with sorrow in his voice.

"Well, none of my other cloths would have fit right anyway, it feels like I am all skin and bones. I take it that you have a plan. I mean my family wants to kill me and I have nowhere else to go. So, what is your plan?" Raven's voice had gone from a normal volume to hysterics by the time she was done talking. Azure clamped his hand over her mouth, and he slid behind Raven to hold a hand over her mouth and circled her waist with the other. He bent his head down just a little and began to talk into her ear.

"Are you crazy do you want to be caught? If you do then I will just turn you over to the guards and forget all about you, and my feelings for you. Forget how you are the only person that can untie the clans. Forget how if your brother takes over than the whole country will be destroyed by his tyranny. Is that what you want?"

He spoke in a normal voice, but she could feel that there was pain in it. Raven not sure if it was from the thought of losing her or the possibility of her brother's evil ruling the world. He held her against him so tightly that she could feel his heart beating. Raven concentrated on his heartbeat and tried to match hers to his. Once Raven calmed down enough, she nodded her head so he would move his hand.

"No, I don't want to be caught and no I don't want my brother to rule if he is as bad as you say he is. Why don't you tell me the history of the clans just the basic information nothing too in-depth." Raven said as she sat down on the bed and stared up at him, waiting for him to speak. He took a deep breath and sat down on the bed and gently took Raven's hand as he began to talk.

"Five brothers were raised by a she wolf and a small pack of other wolves. No one knows where a she wolf got five human kids from, but that is not so important. The boys grew into men and having been raised by wolves avoided human contact. Until one bitterly cold winter day a young woman got separated from her traveling group. The woman had fallen or was knocked off her horse, she hit a sharp rock near the road and was rendered unconscious and needed help. The men felt an odd sense of protectiveness towards her. One of them picked her up and took her back to the cave where they grew up. The young woman regained her senses and slowly regained her health and began to teach the men how to behave as humans. After five years or so the young woman and the men left the forest and began to interact with others. The young woman married one of the brothers and they settled down in Heather Crag. The other brothers lived with them for a while. Eventually they all fell in love and married and formed the five clans. The Wolf Tear clan of Rose Hedge; the Wolf Heart clan of Moon Haven, the Wolf Blood clan of Heather Crag, the Wolf Song clan of Singing Willow, and lastly my clan of Wolf Soul of Oak Heart. The five clans have had their differences through the centuries but in times of trouble they have always stood together. The legend that surrounded the clans was that with the brothers being raised by wolves than they themselves could change into wolves. No one knows why the clans are fighting now. The rumor is that they are tired of being a group rule and feel that one should be above the rest of the clans. Your father is one of the leaders that are trying very hard to pass that ruling. He feels that he should be leader because he is the oldest of the cousins."

Raven sat there dumbfounded after Azure was done talking. She was having a hard time wrapping her head around the fact that a she wolf would raise human children let alone five of them. Then the fact that her father wants to rule everyone it was almost too much. They talked about several other things long into the night. Azure let her sleep on the bed alone just as he had done the night before. He pulled a chair over by the stove and slept there the remainder of the night. Raven's night was full of dreams of men turning into wolves and protecting their families. The wolves were chasing her in a couple of the dreams and in others she was a wolf. Each time she awoke from one of these terrifying dreams she would see Azure sleeping in the chair by the fireplace, and she would feel safe and drift back off to sleep.

Chapter 7

When the day dawned, it was chilly with a hint of frost in the air as well as a heavy fog. It was not cold enough that she would have seen her breath; however, she was glad that she had her cloak. The wind was blowing a little bit and every now and then a large gust would come and try to knock her down.

"Well at least this fog will obscure us from the soldiers some. However, it will make things slow going until it burns off. We might have to walk after sundown to get where we need to go, will you be okay walking after dark?" Azure asked concern lacing his voice

"I often walked after dark when I left my village" She responded.

They figured that it would be less likely to raise suspicious if they acted like they had every right to walk out of the village. As they exited out into the alley, Raven stepped back out of Azure's way so he could lead the way. As they walked out of the alley Azure re-adjusted his pack, and Raven saw that they were right next to the general store. She made sure that her pack was secured as well as her two water skins. Azure turned and walked in front of the store, and they headed out of town. Just when Raven was sure that they were going to make it out of town without any problems, a guard stopped them.

Raven reached up and pulled on her hood just a little bit more to make sure that her hair was covered. She also made sure to keep her head down. While looking down at her feet, Raven was pretty sure that the cloths that she was wearing made her look like any other stable boy. Azure had Raven wrapped some bed sheets around her chest to flatten out her breasts enough to pass as a boy. Azure had very tightly braided her hair and made sure that it was tucked into her cloak. She held her breath slightly as she listened to the guard.

"Where are the two of you going? All servants are to be up at the manor house, you know that the feast is scheduled for tonight." The young guard said in a stern voice

"I wish that we were still employed at the manor house however I was released from my duties. I served the lord the wrong meal the other night, so now I am heading to my village in disgrace. My young friend here was told that he was not to come back until he found that big black mare. Not being able to find it around here anywhere, he was told to travel further and find the mare. Not having the ability to talk he needs someone to travel with, so I am taking him with me and hopefully he will be able to find the horse." As Azure was explain this Raven was intently staring at the guard's shoes, in hopes that he would not really take notice of her.

"Very well then be on your way but know this that our lord does not forget indiscretions against him. Once the war starts every male will be required to fight under our lord's standard." The guard said in a harsh tone

"So, the feast is to decide wither the lord will go to war or not?" Azure asked innocently

"That is correct. Apparently, the lord's daughter was stolen from the tower by a rival clan. In fact, the same clan that the girl was supposed to be married to their eldest son. No one knows for sure how the clan got into the tower let alone how they were able to take to girl out of the manor without anyone noticing. We have been stopping all girls and all wagons leaving the city."

"Ah I understand, well as you see we are both men. I will keep in mind when the lord sends messages calling for the men to come and fight, I will be sure to join up." Azure replied curtly. The guard sent the two of them on their way without any further troubles. They walked in the direction of the meadow.

"I thought that you said we were not going to the meadow?" Raven said with a little confusion in her voice.

"We're not but, the game trail that leads to the caves is off the main road, also there are other things in this direction other than the meadow." He sounded like he was laughing at Raven without laughing at her.

Raven and Azure walked until the sun was high in the sky before they stopped to eat a little of the dried meat and drink some water from their water skins. The fog had long ago burned off and the day was becoming rather warm. Raven had attempted to uncover her head several times; however, every time she would reach up Azure would slap her hand away. She would glare at him out of the corner of her eye.

True to his word they did not head to the meadow. They had gone past the trail that headed to the meadow and at the next trail they headed off the road. The birds were calling and singing back and forth over head was relaxing to Raven's soul. Azure and her traveled in silence they even ate in silence it was a comforting silence. The sun was setting when they stopped at small clearing for the night. There were stumps of all sizes as well as a couple of very large stumps that worked as chairs, Raven sat on one so she could rest her feet. Azure walked around and collected branches and other dead limbs so he could get a fire going.

He pulled up a small area of grass so that the fire was on dirt instead of on the dry grass giving the two of them one less thing to worry about. Azure piled the grass up and struck the flint and steal that he had in his pack to get a fire going. Raven took off her pack and placed it on a smaller stump next to the one that she was using to sit on.

"I am going to go hunt and try to find something for dinner. Why don't you look around here for any editable plants?" Azure said after he got the fire going.

"Okay, but what are you going to use to hunt with you don't have a bow. Unless you are really lucky you won't be able to get close to anything to use your knife." Raven answered. He just grinned at her and headed off into the trees.

Raven kept the fire going in case he did catch something; she looked around for eatable plants in case he didn't. She found some wild onions and some dandelion leaves, Raven figured that they would at least have something to eat. Azure came back about an hour later with two rabbits he had caught, he had skinned, and gutted them along with impaling them on sharpened stick to put over the fire. When the rabbits were done, they ate the greens and onions along with the rabbit.

After all the food was eaten Raven readied their camp area for bed, she untied the bedrolls from their packs, and she laid them down near the fire. As she did that, she noticed that Azure was gathering armloads of wood. Raven figured that he was wanting a good supply of wood for the night. As they were sitting on their bedrolls getting ready to go to bed for the night Azure handed her a leather wrapped box.

"What is this?" Raven asked surprised.

"It is something that I want you to wear all the time after today, it has been in my family for a few generations. It is always given to the oldest male to give to a woman that he loves." He responded with a shy half grin

Raven was speechless. She was almost afraid that she had heard him wrong. Had he just said that he loved her? Her hands began to shake a little bit as she unwrapped the box and opened it. In the box there was an ornate silver hair comb. The top was a half-circle in the center was a trinity knot flanked on both sides by howling wolf heads. The wolf eyes were made of amber and there was an emerald in the center of the knot. In an awed voice Raven said.

"Let me get this straight you love me and if I put this beautiful item in my hair that is me accepting you. Is that right?" As she finished talking, she moved onto his bed roll and looked him in the eyes. He looked a little sheepish and said

"Yes, it means all of that."

Raven grinned and put the comb into her hair. She leaned over and hugged him. As she was hugging him, he gave her a kiss that sent butterflies winging through her stomach. Just as Raven was leaning out of the kiss, she heard a deep angry growl. She opened her eyes and looked over Azure's shoulder. There was a large grey wolf no more than 10 feet away showing its teeth. Raven could tell by the way that its body was hunched that it was about ready to jump; Azure had turned around and was getting ready to get up when the wolf jumped.

Not thinking Raven shoved Azure over and at the same time pulled the comb from her hair in one smooth motion. She slashed the wolf across the muzzle deep enough that the comb drew blood. It yelped and ran off crashing through the underbrush. Azure stood up as if to pursue the wolf. Raven grabbed his hand and tugged a little bit; she was hoping that he understood that she was afraid to be alone. He seemed to fight against staying and charging after the wolf. In the end he decided against pursuing the wolf, he sat down and wrapped his arms around Raven, and they sat like that for a long time. When she was calm and no longer shaking Azure grabbed the comb from her hand and cleaned it, once that was done, he put it back in her hair.

"I am going to suggest that we sleep in shifts in case that wolf comes back." Azure declared.

"Yes, I agree, do you want the first shift, or should I take it?" Raven asked.

"I will take first watch you get some sleep, love." He responded with a caressing look in his eyes.

Raven was so happy she had a hard time falling asleep. When she was finally able to sleep the last thing, she saw was Azure. He was sitting on the other side of the fire looking out into the trees were the wolf fled to. It was about midnight when Azure woke her up, she was a little groggy, but she managed to stay awake until morning. She made sure to put her knife on her side in case the grey wolf came back. Just as the sun was rising Raven could have sworn that she saw a golden wolf about 50 feet into the trees.

She rubbed her eyes thinking that she was seeing things and looked again at where it had been only to discover that it was gone. She dismissed it as her just being tired. She woke Azure up and he went to look for some food to break their fast. While he was gone, she got the fire going again.

Chapter 8

As she was trying to get the kindling to lite when she heard a sound from behind her. She moved her right hand across her belly to the hilt of her knife that was on her left side. Once her hand was on the hilt, she spun around still on her knees with the blade drawn. She came face to face with a golden wolf muzzle right in her face. She was so scared that she froze. Before she could get her hand up to defend herself, she saw a blur, then the wolf and whatever it was that slammed into it hit the ground about 5 feet away.

She saw that it was Azure who had slammed into the wolf. The two were staring at each other and she could swear that she was hearing two different growls happening. The next thing Raven knew there was a bright flash of light, and an older man was on the ground was the golden wolf had been. He looked to be about 6 foot tall standing up. His hair was golden brown and long enough to touch the top of his shoulders. His dark blues eyes looked almost black.

"Lord Markus I did not know that it was you." Azure said as he bowed his head.

"It is understandable. I take it, that this is my daughter?" The old man asked gesturing towards Raven.

"Yes, it is." Azure responded

"If you are my father, why were you a wolf?! Why did you want me, and my mother killed?! What the hell is going on?!" Raven asked rather franticly. She was on the verge of hyperventilating from the rising panic that she was feeling.

Azure stood up slowly and walked backwards over to her, all the while he keeps an eye on Markus. Azure reached his hand down to help her stand. Raven kept a hold of her knife and it pointed at Markus. Azure reached down and took hold of her hand that had the knife and took the knife out of it.

"Raven this is your father Lord Markus of Wolf Tear." Azure said once he had her knife in his belt. He thankfully did not let go of her hand. She was shaking again and felt as if she might shake apart.

"You mean to tell me that the stories of men turning into wolves are true and my father is one of them? Does that mean that I am one of them as well!?" Raven heard herself ask all of this in a quiet and calm voice but in her head, she was screaming these questions at the top of her lungs.

"Yes, I am your father. Yes, when I was younger, I was selfish I did not want to share. Not share my land, my gold, or my clan with anyone. I knew that your mother would not stand for your death, so I went to the healer Key-Na and paid her to kill both of you. I did love your mother, so I asked Key-Na to give your mother a sleeping potion that she would never wake up from. I was a stupid man and I all could think about was my own greed and selfishness. After Key-Na left and your mother was gone I figured that Key-Na had done her job and then left so no one would know about it. It was only after your brother was born that I realized how bad of a choice I had made, I regretted it every day after that. Then one of my guards was told about a woman who looked like my late wife. I told him to find her and bring her to me. I had to know for sure if I had indeed lost my wife or if she and the child had both survived. Your brother must have been listening. He told the guards, to throw you in the dungeon instead of bringing you to me as I had asked. As soon as I heard that you were in the dungeon, I ordered you to be moved to the tower so that I could see and visit with you. When I found out that you had lost consciousness, I asked that one of the maids clean you up and change your cloths. Once I was done with my duties for the day I went to the tower and discovered that you were not there.

Not knowing what had happened I sounded the alarm. My men searched the town and the manor, but no one knew where you had gone. How did you avoid the guards? As for you being a wolf, I am sure that you are. If you were not, then the bite that you received from the gray wolf would have killed you. The main thing that makes the five clans special is the fact that we can decide when we shift from human to wolf. However, we first have to be made aware of our dual nature in order to shift. Your mother should have told you of this when you reached 16 winters old. Why is it that you did not know about any of this? Is your mother still alive? Please tell me that there is a chance that I will be able to see her again." He spoke the last part with such grief and pain in his voice. Raven could tell that he was indeed sorry for what had happened when he was younger. By the time that he had finished talking Raven was sitting on the ground with her hands in her lap.

"Why does my brother want me dead?" She asked afraid of what the answer would be.

"He is worse than I was when I was younger much to my dismay. He has become uncontrollable and dangerous, to anyone who stands up to him. Especially lately it seems that he has times when he becomes crazy and attacks anyone near him. The only person that seems to be able to be around him during these times is his valet, Jerome. His anger is why I was so persistence in finding you after you disappeared. I was worried that he killed you before I could name you as my heir. He wants to rule all the clans any way that he can. Wither that is by killing all the royal family, or by making treaties with them where he is in charge. I truly wish that I had never wanted you or your mother dead. I followed his trail when he left the feast unexpectedly. He followed the two of you and once I smelled blood, I was afraid that he had killed you." He said the last sentence with tears in his eyes.

"No, I pulled the betrothal comb that Azure gave me. I guess that my brother is the big gray wolf. As he jumped, I slashed him across the muzzle. He has attacked me twice now, once before I was taken and then again last night." Raven said calmly with a slight sneer in her voice.

She was so distracted by all the new information that she had been told. She had not even noticed that Azure was no longer by her until he handed her a bowl with some berries and bread in it. She watched as he walked over and covered her father with a blanket. She did not even register that he had been nude the whole time that they had been talking she watched as Azure handed him a bowl as well. Azure sat down by her and draped his arm over her shoulders. Raven's father gazed at him but said nothing. No one spoke until Markus and Raven were done eating. She was the first one to break the silence.

"I have no idea if my mother is still alive or not. If she, is she would be in Rain Rock. Key-Na raised me after I was shunned by the village elders because of my looks. After I turned five winters, I never saw my mother again even from afar. I always figured that she did not want me. So, on another note is everyone in the clans' wolves or just the royal blood lines?" She asked the last question with humor in her voice because it was either cry without stopping or laugh hysterically.

Before anyone could say anything a loud crashing and clanking sounds was suddenly filling the area. It sounded like the woods were filled with soldiers. Before she could do anything more than stand up, her father stood up proud and tall and faced the woods. The guards stepped out in front of Markus; the lead guard stumbled a little as if not excepting to see him. Azure step in front of Raven to the point that she was hidden from view. She was glad that Azure was so broad across the shoulders that his cloak hid her from the guards.

"My lord we were told by your son that you had been killed and that we would find your killers in this clearing. I am confused by what is going on my lord. Your son came to the guard house and called all of us guards to assemble in your office. We saw that he had been clawed across the face by something. So, when he told us that you and he had been out hunting this morning before dawn, and had been attacked by renegades. They came out of nowhere and when you and he tried to flee they killed you by an arrow in the back, and he was slashed across the face with a branch. We figured that he was telling the truth. Because of your death he has claimed the area for himself and has already been made into the clan leader. I am sorry my lord, but you are no longer in charge. I can see that you are alive and in well health. It seems as if you and your friends drove the renegades off, before anyone was hurt more. Unfortunately, you do know the law my lord and that it states that once a new lord is appointed the older lord if still alive can never step foot back in their old territory. We guards will escort you to the edge of the territory along with your friends." The captain said all of this and as he talked his voice took on an uneasy sound.

"That won't be necessary captain. This is young lord Azure of the Wolf Soul clan. He will accompany me across the border and into his territory." Markus spoke with such command and strength.

The guards turned around without another comment and headed back to town. Raven felt like walking with the guards back to town even though she knew that she did not want to go back there. She did not even realize that she had started to move until Azure grabbed her arm to stop her. After she lost sight of the guards, she looked at Azure questionable, Raven was about to open her mouth to ask what had happened when he said.

"Your father has the ability to influence others to do what they really want to do. The guards just wanted to go back to town, so he persuaded them to follow that desire. In doing so however I am not sure why you were affected. Unless your subconscious really wants to go back to town. Do you want to go back?" Azure asked the last part with a hurt tone to his voice.

"No, I really just want to be normal again. I don't want to be a wolf; I don't want to be a royal anything. I want my life simple, I want to heal people, and I want us to be together. Maybe I felt like if I went back to town and told my brother that I did not want to rule he would leave me alone." She finished with a slight pleading sound in her voice. Markus turned and looked her in the eye as he laid a hand on her shoulder and said

"Unfortunately, my child, your brother will never leave you alone. He hates that you are alive, and until you are no longer a threat to him, he will hunt you." He looked at Raven and she could see how upset the thought of her dying at her brother's hands hurt him. Before she could stop herself, she leaned into him and hugged him. Raven decided right then that she would do all she could to get to know her father.

"Well, we should get going before the soldiers come back and check to make sure that we are leaving the area. If we get going right now and not stop, we should be able to make it to my clan's territory by night fall." Azure said as he bent down to pick up his and Raven's pack.

"I don't suppose that you have something for me to wear?" Markus asked

"I thought that you would prefer to travel in your other form for an easier trek through the woods." Azure responded with is playful grin. All Markus did was smirk at him and then there was a blinding light when Raven could see again the golden wolf was back. He took off at an easy lope opposite of Rose Hedge.

"So, are we still going to the cave? Are we going to meet back up with Obsidian again?" Raven asked Azure as they started to walk in the direction that Markus had taken.

"I can change into my other form and get her and have her waiting for you at the border, but I want you father to be with you if I am not."

"Okay so how do I get a hold of him? Should I just howl for him?" She said with a joking sound in her voice.

"Ha-ha very funny. No, I will change forms and send him back to guard you." Azure said as he stopped walking and began to shed his cloths. Raven quickly turned her head so that way she wouldn't get blinded by his light. Also, so she did not embarrass herself by staring at him in all his naked glory. She heard a soft growl from where he had been standing so she turned back to look at him.

Raven saw the most beautiful black wolf standing were Azure had been. He was all black except for a white crescent moon shape on his forehead. He kept his gorgeous Hazel colored eyes in his wolf form. Raven stretched out her hand and touched his black pelt. She was expecting it to be rough and course like that of a dog's pelt. She was pleasantly surprised that it was soft as rabbit fur, and she noticed that there was a strength resonated off of him. She was so tempted to kneel next to him; before she could he took off at a run. Raven did kneel down and collected his cloths and his pack. She was not too happy about having to carry her pack as well as his, but she just could not bring herself to be mad at him.

She had just finished picking everything up when Markus came running at full speed towards her. He started to back pedal to avoid colliding with her, so in the end he had to sit down to finally stop. She yelped a little bit from her shock and ended up sitting on her butt as well. Raven started to laugh at herself; her father had a wolfish grin on his face as well. He reminded her of a dog that she had seen once in town when she was younger. That dog had his tongue hanging out just like her father did and the corners of his mouth were turned up in a gin as well. Raven started to laugh even harder to the point where she had tears coming out from the corners of her eyes.

Once she was able to breathe again, she stood up and shouldered Azure's pack along with her own. She looked at her father and said

"Well let's get going father, from the way I understand it we have a lot of ground to cover and only one day to do it."

She walked off towards where Markus had come from. She and Markus walked all day stopping only long enough to eat and drink a little at midday. Markus kept pace beside her for the most part. He would run off every so often, Raven was never sure if it was to scout ahead or to chase some small animal. He never stayed away for long.

As she walked, she allowed her mind to drift off and review everything that happened to her over the past few weeks. She went over what Azure had told her about the clans' history and how they had been raised by a she wolf. Raven guessed that is what allowed them to change into wolves. She began to wonder if her mother had not abandoned her if she would be able change like Azure and her father. Raven decided to ask her father more about her mother when they camped for the night.

At sunset Raven walked into a large clearing, Azure was already there with Obsidian. Still in his wolfen form, she dropped his pack at his feet and walked towards the mare. Obsidian met her halfway and happily nickered at her, Raven hugged her around her beautiful neck. She heard a twig snap behind her as she turned, she saw that Markus staring at the mare. He gingerly put one paw in front of the other as he approached the mare. Obsidian was standing so still that it looked as if she was made from stone. Raven noticed that as Markus got closer Obsidian began to tremble slightly. Once her father was right in front of the mare Raven stepped aside and let go of her neck. There was a blinding light, and her father was standing in front of Obsidian, he gently placed his hand onto her nose. He acted like she was something that would brake if one applied too much pressure.

"Arian is that you, my love?" When Raven's father asked that question the mare nickered slightly as if she was answering him. Markus fell to his knees his hand still on Obsidian's nose. Raven saw tears sliding down his face, he looked so frail and weak sitting there naked on the ground in front of the mare.

"I am so sorry my love, please forgive me. I am so sorry." He said it so softly, to where if Raven had not been standing by him, she never would have heard him. Obsidian/Arian lay down and nuzzled Markus's cheek almost as if she was accepting his apology.

Raven walked away from Markus and Obsidian she went over to where Azure was standing fully dressed. "I am confused who is Arian? Why does my father think that Obsidian is this Arian?" Raven whispered to Azure after she hugged him. It felt so wonderful to be in Azure's arms again. She almost did not hear what he said in response to her questions.

"Arian is your mother. According to one of the maids that I talked to while you were locked up. The mare showed up a couple of days before you did. Your brother fancies himself an expert horseman. So, when a beautiful pure black horse showed up all of a sudden, he tried to ride it. The mare went crazy as soon as he was on her back. She threw him every time he got on to her back. He became so angry that he allowed his other side to come out and slashed her flank. Once he calmed down the maid overheard him tell his valet Jerome that he was going to go hunt the mare down and kill it. I can only guess that the day that you found her was because she wanted you to. When we found her that day that you brought me to your home, I recognized her scent. I figured that since she was under a spell that I would be able to use that magic to help heal her. I am guessing that your brother found her that day while you were in town and then came back that night to finish the job. However, when he saw you looking so much like your mother you became the subject of his hatred not the mare. I truly think that he was planning on you dying from your wound." By the time that Azure was done talking they were sitting on the grass and her parents were still sitting together. The sun had set, and it was that twilight time of night in between the sun setting and the moon rising. Raven noticed that Markus had found a pair of pants they seemed a little short for his height. Only hitting him about mid-calf, so Raven figured that Azure must have left them out for him to put on.

"We should try to gather some firewood. Even though we are on my clan's land it won't stop your brother from hunting you and your father now. I know that fire won't scare off you brother, but it will help us to see him before he is on top of us." Azure stood up as he was finishing talking.

He held his hand out for Raven without a though she put her hand in his and with his help stood up. Once she was standing, she looked over towards where her parents were at. She did not see them anymore, but she could hear her father talking. She couldn't make out exactly what he was saying but she was able to identify the rhythm and tone of his voice. He seemed to be talking to her mother in a melodious apologetic voice.

After Azure and Raven gathered up some firewood, they got a small fire going nothing too big but enough to shed some light. The mare was still by Markus's side, when they moved over to the fire. Raven noticed that Arian stayed very close to Markus almost as if she felt incomplete without him, she would nuzzle his shoulder with soft nickering. Raven was still trying to wrap her head around the fact that she had a horse for a mother, a wolf for a father, and she loved a wolf. As well as being a wolf herself and having a brother that wanted her dead.

While she sat there, she began to wonder how many more strange things were going to happen to her. It seemed that her life had become one of the myths that she had read about in Key-Na's books. Raven was spooked from her reminiscing by the sound of a deep growl and a very shrill whinny. She looked over towards where her parents were sitting in time to see three smallish black wolves attack her parents. Two jumped on her father and the third jumped on to her mother's back snapping at her neck. Azure stood and began to yell.

"NO, STOP!! THEY ARE UNDER MY PROTECTION."

Raven jumped to her feet and leaped over the fire in an effort to protect her parents. She grabbed ahold of the wolf on her mother's back with both hands at the scruff of its neck. Raven's fingers dug in deep and tried to pull the wolf off, instead she received a bite to her forearm. Raven screamed in pain she released the wolf. Before the wolf could bite her again Azure was jumping on to the back of the wolf in his wolf form. Raven saw that Azure had clamped his jaws down on the back of the neck hard enough to cause the wolf to let out a loud howl in pain. The wolf stayed on its side at Azure's feet. Raven watched the other two wolves come charging at Azure looking to be all teeth and claws. However, before the reached him, Azure changed back into his human form and grabbed them both by the throat as they jumped towards him. He then tossed both away from him. The look on his face caused a shiver of fear to race down Raven's spine. She hoped that he would never look at her the way he looked at the wolves. He shouted with a deep growl in his voice

"I SAID ENOUGH!!! NOW BACK DOWN!!!"

The three young wolves changed into 3 boys that all looked rather ashamed. They all looked like Azure but younger. Raven watched Azure grabbed some rope from the packs and tossed it to Markus to tie the boys up. After the fight Azure wrapped her arm up, as well as Markus's arm. After Markus tied the boys up. Arian's neck wound from what Raven could see looked really bad. Azure had to use his magic to heal the bite. Once the boys were tied up Azure placed them across the fire pit from the four of them. Raven was leaned against her mother's, Arian, side; she could feel Markus standing behind the two of them. She felt rage rolling off of her father it was so intense that it made her stomach nauseous. Azure was sitting next to Raven holding her hand, glaring at the boys.

Chapter 9

The three boys had shirts on that Raven asked Azure to give them because she was not very comfortable with their nakedness. The shirts hung past their knees Azure untied each boy put the shirt on them and then retied the ropes. Once they were clothed and retied, Azure pointed to the ground and each one of the boys sat on the ground. Every once and awhile Raven would hear a growl from Azure directed at the boys, but he did not go near them.

She got up and walked over to her bag and pulled out the honey, some cloth, and a few herbs. She also grabbed out one of the bowls and began to mix the herbs and honey together and set it close to the fire. After the honey warmed up a bit, she was able to mix it into a sticky paste. She applied the mix to the cloth and walked over to her father. She unwound the wrap that Azure had done and applied half of the mixture on to the gash that he had on his arm. He hissed a little from the pain as she put the bandage back on tightly.

She then handed the bowl to her father. She unwrapped her arm and waited for him to apply the mixture to her bite. Her father smeared the mix onto her arm and once done he wrapped her arm back up. When Markus was done with her bandage, she took the bowl back and made a mental note to wash it the next day. She put it back in her bag and then she sat back down next to Azure. It was all she could do not to stare accusingly at the boys across from her so instead she stared into the fire. They had almost cost her everything. Raven thought the only reason why the boys were still alive is because they were Azure's younger brothers.

"We didn't know that you were with them all we knew was that he was in our territory." The taller one stated in a slightly whinny voice nodding towards Markus.

"We felt him cross the border along with some other wolf. We thought that it was an attack." The smallest one sounded even more whining than tall one.

"I don't care what you felt Draco!!! Since when are the three of you on guard duty anyway?! You three are barely old enough to shift let alone attacking anyone. Why did you not inform mother or father or even the guards?" Azure demanded rather forcefully.

"Beo and Oryeon didn't want them to know. They thought that the three of us were old enough to handle it." Draco replied in slightly less whinny voice.

Azure walked around the fire to untie the three boys. The three of them stood as one and waited. Raven was surprised at how the three of them seemed to move as one she then watched them turn as if to walk away. Raven heard a growl and saw Azure once again point to the ground the boys sat back down in unison. There was another growl this time it sounded louder and more of a reprimand; the boys all looked at the ground. Azure let out a huff of air and looked at Raven.

"These are my younger brothers they were all born at the same time. The tallest one is called Oryeon, and he is the oldest, the shortest is Draco he is the youngest, the other is called Beo. Draco can feel when different wolves from other clans enter our territory. Wolves that are not part of our clan have a slightly different feel to their magic. Oryeon can make the rains come, that is why we have not had a drought for the past 16 years. And lastly Beo has an amazing mind for planning out attacks and strategies. Believe me you never want to play chess with him, he will make you think you are winning and then he will checkmate you in fewer than three moves." By the time that Azure was done talking he was sitting by Raven holding her hand. She was surprised at the amount of love that he had in his voice even though he was still very upset at the boys.

"As for what lord Markus is doing in our land his son has exiled him through trickery. This lovely woman by my side is, my wife to be and, lord Markus's rightful heir. As you can well imagine her brother is not happy about that. The mare is the Lady Arian. We believe that she is under a spell to make her invisible to the young lord. Draco can you feel what kind of spell was used on her. I believe that everyone here would love to know what happened to her." Azure stated in a matter-of-fact voice.

Draco slowly stood up and walked around the fire. Raven watched him, he seemed rather skittish around Markus. Almost as if he thought that Markus would take a bite out of him. He gently placed a shaking hand against Arian's nose closed his eyes and breathed out in a slow steady breath. Raven watched his face as countless emotions flew over it before contorting in a look of pain. His eyes flew open, and he became stiff as a board. If Markus had not caught him Draco would have landed hard on the ground. Raven was on her feet and moving before her brain registered everything going on.

Raven saw that Markus cradled Draco in his lap and Arian got up moved away her body covered in a fine sheen of sweat almost like she had been running along distance. Raven glanced over her shoulder to Azure and saw that he was holding his other two brothers who seemed to have collapse like Draco. Raven touched Draco's head and found that it was cool his eyes had closed so she had to open them to look. His eyes seemed to have an unfocused look about them. She picked up his arm and it fell limply back down to his side. If she had not seen the way he acted, mere seconds ago, Raven would have said that he was just sleeping. She stood and walked over to check on the other two. She noticed that Azure had laid them down near the fire. Their bodies reacted the same as their brother's body. She was very confused as to what had happened it was like they all just fell asleep. She could hear Azure nearby talking to Arian if she had to make a guess. Markus was still holding Draco she could just make out Arian at the edge of the fire light behind Markus.

She was looking between the three boys when suddenly she was hit from behind by something very large. It hit her so hard that she flew over the fire and away from everyone. She felt a sudden impact on her forehead and before she lost consciousness, she heard loud growls and a shrill whinny, then everything went black.

Chapter 10

When Raven became started to wake up her whole body was a constant throb however her head hurt the most. She hurt so badly that she was sure that at least 3 heavy carts had been driven over her. She could smell meat cooking as well as something sweet and herby nearby, but she could not place where it was the smells seemed to surround her. She also noticed that she was warm, however she could not focus on any one thought because of the pain. Raven decided that to get away from the hurt she would go back to sleep. It worked in the dungeon so why shouldn't it work now.

When Raven woke next, she was pain free and there was a warm light shining on her face. She became aware of a couple of things right away. One was that she could hear people talking nearby and the other was that she was on something soft. She opened her eyes and was blinded by the light; she quickly closed them and turned her head to the side before she opened them again. She was looking at a beautiful tapestry hanging on a dark wooden wall, it was a picture of a tree and on every branch and leaf there seemed to be something written on them. The writing was so small that she could not tell what it said. She continued to look around without turning her head. There was a rather stout light-colored door that could be barred from the inside next to the tapestry.

There was a beat-up looking trunk on the floor on the other side of the tapestry that looked to be of a rather good size. She could see the edge of a rug that looked to be next to the bed going towards the door it was a rich wine red in color, so it stood out from the dark wood floor. Raven closed her eyes so that she would not be blinded again and turned her face to the other side of the bed. When she slowly opened her eyes allowing them to adjust to the light, she saw that there were two chairs near a cold fireplace. The light was from outside streaming through the large window near the fireplace. She could see the edge of the same rug extend towards the fireplace.

She moved her head enough to look at the bed that she was laying on. She saw that the cover was the same wine red as the rug. It also was the biggest bed she had ever been in. There was plenty of room she figured you could easily fit two people on it with room to spare. The pillow next to her was covered in a rich golden fabric that looked extremely soft. Her hand ached to touch it, but she was too comfortable under the blanket to really move. Looking around there did not seem to be anyone in the room yet Raven was still hearing a conversation. She turned her head back towards the door.

She laid there listen to what sounded like a man and a woman arguing on the other side of the door. She could not make out what was being said only that the tones that were being used did not sound very happy. Raven heard the doorknob turn, she quickly closed her eyes and acted like she was still asleep. She decided to get as much information as she could before anyone realized that she was awake. She heard the door open and close quietly then soft foot falls that sounded like they were going over to the chairs. Raven then heard one of the chairs give a soft little groan as someone sat down, and then she heard the door open and close again not as quietly as before.

"Has she woken up at all Azure?"

"No, Markus, she is still sleeping. I know that my mother feels terrible about what she did, however if you had seen your children out cold and some strange person hovering over two of them and another Clan leader holding the third what would you have done?" Azure's voice held a note of question and regret.

"It depends on which of my children." Markus replied with a little bit of laughter in his voice. "If it was Raven then yes in a heartbeat, I did not know how much she would mean to me. I never should have done what I did, and now her mother and her both seem to have forgiven me. However, I cannot forgive myself, I was so blind" Raven heard his voice crack at the end, and she could no longer help herself she opened my eyes and looked at him.

He was standing just inside the door he had his hair pulled away from his face and his cloths made him look every bit of a lord as his title suggested. He was wearing deep blue shirt and a rich earth brown color pants that looked as if they were made just for him. He carried a sword on his left hip and a dagger on his right. He was looking at the floor as if he was too ashamed to look at the bed where Raven was laying.

"Father is that you?" She asked softly whispered she had not known that it would hurt her throat so badly to talk. He looked up with a look of shock on his face just before it crumbled in on itself and he began to cry. She could hear Azure move the chair and walk over to the bed. When she turned her head to look at him all she saw was love beaming in his eyes.

"Are you okay? Do you need anything? Do you hurt anywhere?" Azure asked with heavy concern in his voice.

"I really could use something to drink my throat hurts a lot." Raven was able to hoarsely whisper.

"Of course, I always forget the water." He said laughing at his own joke.

Raven was staring at Azure when she heard the door open and close again, she looked over to where her father had been standing and saw that he was no longer there. She looked back at Azure when she felt the bed dip from him climbing on to it. He wrapped his arms around her and pulled her close. Raven lost track of how long they laid like that, it felt so wonderful to be in his arms. That she forgot about everything else. She did not even notice when her father came back into the room until he cleared his throat.

Azure released her with a chuckle; she sheepishly smiled at her father and sat up as she took the goblet he offered. It smelled like berries and sage along with some honey it was both wonderful tasting and smelling. It helped her throat feel less scratchy and less raw. She was so grateful to finally have something to drink that once she drank half of it before she felt she could talk without pain.

"Who made the tea it was wonderful." She asked looking at her father.

"Your mother made it. The spell on her was broken when she went after Azure's mother for attacking you. We are not sure why exactly, but she is free. The best that Azure and his family can theorize is that the spell was designed that when Arian saw her only child that she loves dearly in mortal danger her wolf side would override the spell and break it." Markus said as he sat at the foot of the bed.

Raven looked at the tea again took another drink and enjoyed it even more than the first drink. She was torn about her mother. Her mind kept running over the same questions again and again. "Why was there a spell on my mother? Who put the spell on her? Why when before when my brother attacked me did, she not anything? Why did she give me up for Key-Na to raise me? Did she hate me because my father wanted me dead and her as well for carrying me?" Raven had so many questions that she was not paying any attention to what was going on around her. As she was thinking she kept drinking the tea. When she took the last drink, she realized that she was alone in her room, but she could hear two men arguing out in the hall.

"SHE IS MY DAUGHTER AND I WILL NOT LET HER REMAIN IN DANGER!" Raven could identify her father's voice yelling in anger.

"THAT MAYBE MARKUS BUT SHE AGREED TO MARRY ME! MY FAMILY PROTECT THEIR OWN UNLIKE SOME ONE I COULD NAME! YOU CHOSE TO HAVE HER KILLED INSTEAD OF SHARING YOUR POWER! NOW YOUR BASTARD IS IN CHARGE AND OUT FOR HER BLOOD!" Azure responded in just as loud of a voice

"I already was forgiven for that mistake by her and her mother. Even though I know that I am unworthy of their forgiveness." Markus's voice held sorrow in it, and it was at a lower volume than before. Even at the lower volume Raven was still able to hear him very clearly.

"That maybe. However, it is different from me forgiving you. She was betrothed to me before she was born, and I grieved for her once I was told about her death. She was a child of the wolf, and you chose to kill her before she even drew her first breath. I grieved for her not just as a mate that had been lost but as a child of the wolf taken before her time. Your greed and fear drove you to try and kill her nothing else. My parents waited until I became old enough to understand what had happened. She was supposed to be mine and I vowed that you would pay for her death. She chose to be mine after all this time, despite what you tried to do. Now I have granted you sanctuary in my lands but do not think for a minute that I forgive you right now. She was shunned by those that were bound by oath to protect the royal family. Yet her mother was so afraid of you that she hid the truth. Where were you during that time? You were in your keep taking liberties with any female that allowed you between their legs. As it is the fruit of your loins, even though he is a bastard, is now in charge of your clan. Goodness only knows what is in store for all of us now. He no doubt has been told by the captain that you crossed into our lands and that I granted you passage." Azure's voice had become quieter, but it dripped with venom and disapproval.

"I understand your hate towards me. I have already told your parents that I will leave. I just ask that I be allowed to remain until you and Raven are married." Markus said the last part in a normal volume.

"No, I will not allow you to leave even after the wedding, my lord. Before you start to argue with me on this as well, let me explain. I want you to try and get to know your daughter and hopefully you will be able to get to know your wife again as well. The reason for this is because you knew who I was and yet you never once demanded to know why I was in your territory. Even though according to our laws you would have been with in your rights to do so. Our biggest concern currently is your son. Do you think that he would use you being in our territory as a sign of war? Do you think that he could rally the other clans to attack us?" Azure's voice was normal volume. Raven got up to move closer to the door to continue to listen into the conversation as they moved away from the door.

"I wish that I could look you in the eye and tell you that he will not attack. I wish I could say that he will not have the other clans declare war on you, but I cannot. In truth I don't even know him any more I have not known him for a few years now." Raven could hear how upset her father was and it made her heart hurt. She opened the door quickly glanced around to see where they were and then threw herself into her father's arms circling his chest in a hug. It seemed to shock him for a moment and then he was hugging her as well. It felt so good to have her father's arms around her and then when Azure began to rub small circles across her back, her world felt almost perfect. She stepped back away from her father and instantly Azure's arms encircled her waist.

"I heard the two of you auguring out here and I have a couple of questions for both of you. So why don't we all either step into the room I am using or find a quiet place that we can talk without being disturbed." As she spoke Raven leaned her back into Azure's chest, she felt so safe standing between the two of them. Raven realized that if her brother attacked her right then that she would be totally safe.

Before either of them could say anything, Raven heard a sharp intake of breath from behind her father. She looked past him and saw the most beautiful woman she had ever seen. The woman was tall and curvy she had black and silver striped hair much like Raven's own. Her skin was not tanned like Raven's. Raven figure she was always going to be tanned she was always outside. The woman's skin was a pale cream as if she had bathed in fresh cream. Raven touched her lips noticing that the woman's mouth was small and nothing like her full lips. The woman's eyes were the golden color that whispering aspens take on every autumn. As Raven looked at her eyes, memories began to flood her mind. Those same eyes looking down at her filled with love and a little bit of fear. The same eyes being lite and dancing with laughter.

Suddenly memories flooded her mind things long buried and lost to her. The last memory that flooded her mind was her looking over her shoulder as her mother was kneeling in the road with seven or eight men behind her all with a very stern and irritated looks on their faces. Two of the men had their hands on her shoulders as if they were forcing her to remain on the ground. Her cloths were dirty and torn as if she had been attacked. There were tears trailing down her face leaving tracks of their passing through the dirt on her face. There looked to be blood near her mouth. Raven did not understand what was going on in her memory. Only that someone was holding her and that her arms were wrapped around that person's neck. She felt alone but at the same time safe.

Raven did not even know that she had those memories she always thought that she was unwanted. However, with that last memory she was able to realize that her mother didn't abandon her. Now her mother was standing not five feet from her, looking at her with love and fear in her eyes. Raven walked out of Azure's arms around her father and slowly walked over to her, not knowing what to say.

"I guess that you have a lot of questions for me Raven. I will answer all that I can, and I hope that one day you will forgive me for the harm that I have done to you." Arian quietly said. It was almost as if she was afraid to talk to Raven.

"No, only one. Why? Why did you ignore me? Why did you avoid me and why did you allow another to raise me? Why?" Raven asked her with tears threating to choke her and spill from her eyes.

"I think we should talk in your room love; this is going to be a lengthy conversation and I don't want the staff to hear any more of the drama." Azure said as he grabbed her hand and began to gently pull her back to the room.

Once all of them were in the room Markus closed the door and walked over to the fireplace Raven watched as her father got a fire going, she figured it was just so he had something to do. Raven's mother sat very straight in one of the chairs facing the bed and Azure and Raven sat on the edge of the bed he refused to let go of her hand. The silence and tension were so thick that it felt like a living thing in the room with them. Her mother broke the silence first.

"I did not ignore you I was forced to hide how much I loved and cared for you. The village that Key-Na and I fled to was in a different territory even though it was right on the edge of the boarder I did not want them to really start to look at me or you. Then your father negotiated for that small amount of land to increase his clans land and we were under his rule. I was afraid that Markus would come and check his new lands, so I changed my name, and always had Key-Na color my hair to hide the silver. I had asked that if Markus ever sent word that he was coming to visit that Key-Na would raise you. I figured that she lived outside of town, and everyone avoided her anyway that it would be the safest place for you to be. Then you changed out of sheer fear at age four and a village elder saw you. I had always told them that you were a foundling, so I was forced to make a choice either I let a witch raise you because that is what you had to be, or I watch you die. It broke my heart to allow Key-Na to raise you but at least I knew that you were alive. Then when you were five years old, I heard that Markus was coming to the village I panicked and begged Key-Na to cast a spell on me. I knew that it took a toll on her, but I was so afraid that your father would recognize me and order me killed again just as he had before." Her voice broke and she was crying Markus turned slightly and placed his hands on to her shoulders and Raven noticed that he began to rub in small circles. It reminded her of what Azure had done. She took a couple of deep breaths and she once she was calm enough to talk, she began again.

"I knew that Key-Na was able to cast spells to change a person into something else. She would use a little magic whenever she helped someone. The magic helped to speed the healing up. However, most of the time she allowed the herbs to take care of the healing on their own. I went to her and told her that I needed to hide but that I needed to stay around you to make sure that you were safe. She said that the spell would only be able to be broken if you were in a life threating situation. I was too weak when your brother attacked you to protect you. When I heard the guards in the woods I hid, I figured that they were from your brother looking for me. When I came back and found you gone, I raced to town in hopes that Azure would be on his way back. When I found him, he guessed that something had happened by the way that I was acting. He changed and ran to the meadow I guided the donkey and cart back home, by the time I got back Azure was freaking out because you had been taken. He left the meadow after he unloaded the cart and turned the donkey loose. I did not see him again until after he found you and took me to the caverns for a safe place. You know the rest."

Raven sat there for a long time looking between her parents. She was not sure what to believe. Raven did know one thing for sure, that was that both her parents cared for her, and they cared for each other. Raven opened and closed her mouth a few times trying to find the right words to say. Everything that she could think to say just didn't sound right or enough. Azure seeing her problem spoke up for her.

"I think that Raven needs time to wrap her head around everything that she has learned. It is a lot of new understanding and things put into a new light. Markus why don't you take Arian back to the room that you are sharing."

He said everything in a calm voice that was so much different than how Raven was feeling. Her mind was in a tornado with all the new information that she had just received. She felt the bed move as Azure got up and she heard him walk her parents to the door. After her parents left Azure sat back down next to her and took her hand. They sat like that a long time the only time that he moved was when he placed her silver betrothal comb back into her hair. She felt the weight of it above her ear but other than that she kept her mind blank in hopes to slowly understand everything and not allow her thoughts to become a tornado again. Every now and then he would give her a light squeeze to remind her that he was there if she wanted to talk. Raven was not sure how long they sat there on the bed as she tried to figure things out. Before she could get it, all sorted however there was a loud persistent knocking on the door. It was then that Raven and Azure noticed that there was screaming coming from somewhere.

Raven jumped off the bed and rushed to open the door Azure was barely a half step behind her. As she opened the door Raven was looking at a young servant girl with tears in her eyes.

"Are you the healer?" she asked frantically as she fought back sobs.

"I know of some healing, yes. Tell me what is wrong." Raven was thankful to have something familiar to deal with.

"It is my brother he was patrolling the boarder and was set upon by something. He was able to remain in his saddle and turn the horse to home. However, once he reached the bailey, he fell unconscious from the horse." As the girl got the last words out, she broke down in great heaving sobs.

Azure grabbed Raven's hand and they raced down the hall to the stairs, and down into the great hall. She noticed that a body had been placed on one of the long tables and it had been set close to the fire. She set her shoulders back and with the appearance of more confidence than what she truly felt, walked over to see how badly the boy had been hurt. It was horrible whatever or whoever had attacked him had torn his chest to pieces. There was so much damage Raven was surprised that he had not expired from blood loss.

"I need clean hot water, rags, bandages, Witch Hazel, Chamomile, Honey and some bayberry if someone can find it. Does anyone else have any knowledge of healing?" Raven asked glancing around the great hall ringing with authority.

"I used to help the healer" Raven's mother said as she stepped away from the crowd that had gathered.

Before Raven's mother was done talking Raven noticed a large pot was placed over the fire and serving boys began to run back and forth from outside to the pot with buckets full of water. A young girl ran with a large basket full of bandages and a younger boy had his hands full with a basket for rags. Another serving girl came running with a large basket full of the herbs that Raven had requested. A small boy was behind her carrying a crock of honey that was almost as big as him. Once the baskets were on the table Raven saw Arian disappeared toward where the girls had come from and returned shortly afterwards with a large wooden bowl. She went over to the pot and filled the bowl with water.

Raven grabbed a rag and dipped it into the hot water and began to clean all the blood off the young man's body. Once all the blood was gone, she was able to see how bad the damage was. There was a large gash across his chest like what Arian had on her flank when she was the mare. There was also a large bite on his arm much like what would happen if he had put his arm up to protect himself. When she was done with cleaning the wounds and then sewing them up, she applied the herbal honey compounds that her mother had been making with Raven's directions. Raven was glad that the young man remained unconscious the whole time that he was being worked on. When she was ready to wrap the bandages around the wounds, she signaled for two of the guards to help hold him up. So that way she would be able to tightly wrap him up to prevent excessive bleeding. She had lost track of how long it had taken her to take care of the young man.

When she was satisfied that he would not bleed all over the place she asked the same guards to help move him to his home. The serving girl that told Raven of her brother's accident showed the guards where they lived. Before he was moved out of the main hall, she told the young woman to get her right away if her brother starts to have a fever or begins to bleed excessively. After he was removed Raven realized that her back and shoulders were bothering her. Especially her right shoulder it was starting to have a constant sting to it.

Raven sat down on the bench closest to the hearth. She had not realized that Azure had followed her or was even still in the great hall she had been so absorbed in her work. As she sat, she looked around the room. It was large with stones mortared closely together. It did have large windows that had thick wooden shutters flaking either side of the window. The fireplace was located near the back of the room it was larger enough to roast a full-grown pig in. there were benches and small tables scattered around the room. The floor was stone it smelled as if the rushes had recently been changed. While she was sitting looking around the room Azure had begun to rub her shoulders to try and loosen the muscles. Every time he applied pressure on her right shoulder, she had to bite back a whimper of pain.

"Azure what would cause a wound on us not to heal correctly?" she asked when she grabbed his right hand to stop him from continuing to rub her shoulder.

"Silver is really the only thing that can cause that kind of problem. Silver is to us how poison is to humans. Our bodies can survive it in some ways, and we can die from it in other ways. For example, if a piece of silver gets into the muscle or bone it will prevent a wound from healing, however if the silver gets into our lungs or heart, we stop being able to breath there by dying from suffocation. In the heart it causes the heart to stop working. Why do you ask?" He asked with concern in his voice.

"I think that if silver is the only thing that can harm us, I must have some in this shoulder wound because it refuses to heal right and it is causing me pain." Raven responded

"It is possible however I am not sure how you would have gotten silver in the wound I cleaned it myself. Your brother's teeth tore into your shoulder muscle, but he did not have enough time to insert anything." Azure had a puzzled sound in his voice

"Can a wolf carry silver, and not be affected by it?"

"I guess it is possible but only for short amounts of time otherwise they would become poisoned." As he spoke the last bit, he sat down by her on the bench and took her hand concern written all over his face.

"Is there any way that we can know for sure if there is silver in the wound? Other than reopening it?"

"I am not sure; we would have to talk to our clan healer however right now he is attending a birthing out in our furthest village. It will take at least a fortnight before he will be back. Can you not tell if there is silver in the wound?" he asked it so sweetly that Raven felt foolish.

"No unfortunately, I can't tell I just know that it is not healing properly. You have a male healer that helps with birthing? How amazing I though only women could become healers." Raven held a note of awe in her voice when she was done talking.

"He is Key-Na's son Cor. I guess that his mother's healing ability flow in the blood. He is very smart. The reason that he is with us instead of with your father's clan is because, when Key-Na decided to save you and your mother she sent him to us so your father could not harm him. She knew that our healer had died the previous summer and that the clan needed a skilled healer."

"By the way something has been bothering me. How were you able to mourn me before I was born?" Raven asked inquisitively

"You heard your father and I arguing, didn't you?" Azure bowed his head in shame as he asked his question.

Raven placed her hand under his chin and smiled at him and replied, "Yes I did, now please tell me."

"Key-Na had sent for my mother when I was about 4. My mother told me to wait outside she needed to have a woman only conversation. Well, being curious I listened at the window it was open very little but enough that I heard the prophecy that Key-Na had found. From what I can remember of the prophecy it was something along the lines of…

"When oaken heart meets rosy hedge then the two shall be wed. When bitter cold, seeks bitter blood, then the two, shall bleed as one. Once spring is sprung again, tyranny shall meet its own end. Finally, the five in lasting harmony, free of tyranny's greed and sin."

After Key-Na told my mother this they began to talk of things that a young boy should not hear. I saw a cherry tree at the edge of the meadow and decided that I could climb up and get the last cherries that where at the top of the tree. Instead, about halfway up I startled a bird and with its wings flapping in my face I lost my balance and fell out of the tree, breaking my arm. I always thought that I had missed out on have a lifelong friend, when my father told us that Lady Arian had died. It was only after I became a teenager that my parents told me that you were to be my betrothed. I did not want you to think that I helped you just so that I could force you into becoming my mate. I really do care for you Raven with all of my being and I truly hope that you care for me and can forgive me for withholding parts of the truth from you." he said the last part on his knees in front of Raven and she could see his hope and love shining in his eyes. She leaned down and kissed him.

"I could never be upset at you; you saved my life more times than I care to count." She whispered softly

Before he could say anything, they heard someone clearing their throat. The two of them looked up and saw her parents and a couple that she did not recognize. Raven's parents were holding hands and smiling at Azure and her. The other couple looked to be Azure's parents.

The woman was tall around 6 feet tall or so she reminded Raven of a young willow because she was so tall and thin. Her skin was so pale that it looked like she had never been out in the sun. She also had pale, almost white, blond hair it hung down her back loosely about three inches off the floor. Her eyes were aqua green and large in comparison to her face.

"My name is Leena, and I am Azure's mother. This man beside me is my mate Griffin he is lord of the Wolf Soul clan." She said is a calm and authoritative voice. It reminded Raven of the sound of bells on a crisp winter morning.

Raven looked at Griffin and understood where Azure got his looks from. Griffin was a tall and muscular man with thick raven black hair that brushed the middle of his shoulders he wore it loose around his face. His laughing steel grey eyes reminded her of how the sky looks just before a storm. He stood as tall as Leena and where her skin was snow white his was tan from working in the sun.

"I gather that you and my son will be wed as was arranged in the marriage contract?" Griffin asked his voice carried authority without even having to raise his voice.

Azure stood slowly and pulled Raven up with him. He placed himself in between her and his father as if he was protecting her from Griffin. With him shielding her, she reached up and pulled the comb out of her hair. Once she had it in her hand she boldly stepped around Azure and showed the room the comb.

"I have accepted Azure's love gift and yes we are going to be wed, however it is not out of duty to a contract it is out of pure love and trust. If that is unacceptable to anyone in this room than I will leave. I am tired of not being in control of my own life and my own choices." Raven spoke and then realized that everything that she had just said was true. "I love Azure but ever since I walked away from the only home that I ever knew. My choices have not been my own on more than one occasion I chose who I marry, and I chose how I am to live."

Azure stepped up next to her and grabbed her hand firmly and said in a voice that boomed around the great hall with sheer power.

"This is my mate. I claim her before all that are present. She is my only reason for living. My honor is hers as her honor is mine. She is my soul as I am her soul. We are one from this day forward and if anyone says nay let them speak now." he spoke with such forcefulness his mother took a step back.

Before Raven knew what was happening it was over and everyone other than their parents were standing. She looked at her parents, Markus had an odd look on his face almost as if he could not believe what just happened. Arian eyes were shinning from unshed tears. Seeing how her parents reacted Raven looked at Azure's parents. Leena looked upset much like she had just taken a mouth full of something sour. Griffin however looked very proud of what had just happened. Azure took the comb from her hand and pulled out a gold bracelet from his belt pouch. It looked too small for her but as he went to slide it one, it grew around her hand and then formed to her wrist.

"This is a very old gift it changes shape to fit the wearer no matter what. You are now my mate and where you go, I go no matter what." Azure was almost beaming from pride at the fact that Raven was now and forever his.

As she gazed at the bracelet, she heard what sounded like stomping. Raven looked up and saw Lady Leena storming off, her back being ramrod straight and she was almost vibrating from the anger that was pouring from her. Griffin was just watching his mate storm off Raven could not tell if he was covering his mouth to hide a smile or if he was perplexed as to what to do. Raven didn't have any more time to wonder about it because she was suddenly enclosed in a very large hug from both her mother and father. The rest of the afternoon and into the evening passed in a blur, between all the congratulations and the feasting and other merry making. Raven was so tired by the time that it was dark out that all she wanted to do was crawl into bed and sleep for a week.

When they got back to their room Raven realized that she was feeling shy and slightly afraid. Raven knew what was about to happen but that did not calm her down any. The door didn't even close all the way before there was a loud knocking on it. Raven looked at Azure and saw him roll his eyes as he blew out his breath and turned and opened the door.

"I am sorry to disturb you on your wedding night lord, but it is your turn on guard duty and patrol." Raven heard a crisp voice from the hall.

"I forgot that I was due on that tonight." Azure said exasperated "I will be there is a few minutes officer." Azure replied as he closed the door.

"Well love it looks like I have other duties tonight but there is always tomorrow." He had a mischievous look in his eyes as he leaned in for a kiss. As his lips met hers there was another loud banging on the door.

They broke apart he turned back to the door, and she walked over to the bed, which was when she noticed that there was a sheer sleeping gown laying on it. Knowing that it was not there before Raven figured that her mother had placed it there as a wedding present. As she was admiring the gown, she heard Azure thank someone and close the door. She was about to turn around to ask what that was about, when strong arms encircled around her waist and pulled her up close to someone chest. She briefly froze from fright then she recognized Azure's scent and leaned into him. About that time exhaustion caught up with her, and she fell asleep standing in his arms.

Chapter 11

Raven was startled awake by a loud mournful howl. The room was totally dark. Raven noticed that she was wearing the same gown that she had worn the day before. She also noticed that she was not alone in the room or alone in the bed. Azure was sitting up staring at her. When there was no sound Raven thought that she had just imagined the howl until she heard it again. As the last howl died off another howl started. The howls tore at Raven's very soul she knew that something horrible had happened. Azure howled at that moment.

"What is going on" Raven asked in a shaking voice. Before she received and answer she felt a searing pain in her chest, the pain forced her to howl out in pain. She heard running feet in the hall and the door suddenly swung open.

"Lord Azure, Lady Raven come to the great hall now! HURRY!!!!" Raven could not tell who it was that hollered but she could sense the need to hurry.

When she reached the great hall, she was out of breath and her heart was pounding so fast that she could have sworn it had grown to encompass her whole body. She paused long enough at the top of the stairs to see that there was a large group of people in the center of the hall all clustered in the center around something.

When Raven reached the bottom of the stairs, she began pushing her way through the group. She had no logical reason to reach the center of the hall she just knew that she had to. When she reached the center, she dropped to her knees from shock. On a long cart were the remains of Griffin and Markus. They had been torn to shreds their bodies were cover in horrendous bites that went all the way to the bone. In some places the bones were even missing. Raven could tell that whatever had attacked the two lords wanted people to recognize them as their faces were untouched in any way.

Raven felt some one step close to her; she looked up and saw that it was Azure. He had a look on his face that she had never seen on any one before. He helped Raven stand up but did not acknowledge her other than that. He held her hand and every now and then he would squeeze it to let her know that he knew she was still there. After a few minutes Azure closed his eyes tipped his head back and emitted a mournful howl. Raven could tell that Lady Leena and the boys joined in by the high pitch and three softer howls joined Azure in his sorrow. The great hall rang from all the howls, it caused so much pain that all the people that had been standing around began to wail from the overwhelming sense of grief.

As their howls died down over the wailing, Raven heard a single howl that warbled ever so slightly as if someone's voice had not howled in a long time. She looked up toward the sound and saw her mother standing on the stairs. She could see that her head was tipped back and that there were tears on her face. Raven glanced over at Azure's mother and saw the tears in her eyes, but she refused to shed them. The boys all had tears running down their faces. Before Raven's mother's howl ended Raven tipped her head back howled from her grief and pain.

She felt so hurt and sad that her body began to burn all over. She doubled over and fell to the floor. Everything became hazy shapes that blurred, and the colors ran together. It felt as if someone had poured fire over Raven's body, then threw her into ice water. The pain was so great that she was sure that she would pass out. Just when she was about to everything stopped. The pain stopped, the imagines became clear again and colors were sharper, the stench of death was overpowering.

Raven tried to stand up but couldn't get her body to work the right way. She looked up at Azure and saw that he had a surprised look on his face. As she went to put her hands down to help push herself up, she saw that instead of hands she had white paws. Her body began to tremble as she saw that her gown was pooled around her on the floor. Azure knelt and placed his hand on her head.

"You are so beautiful wife; I had no idea that you were pure white." Azure sounded in awe of Raven's coloring

She tried to talk and instead all that happened was she let out a whine. Raven was confused as to what happened. She could tell that her heart still hurt, but at the same time it was like she could deal with it. She looked over to where her mother had been standing and in her place was a brown wolf with a white star on her forehead. The she wolf looked at her and then started down the stairs. Raven stayed where she was; she really was not sure how to move in her new body.

When Arian reached Raven, she rubbed her body against her, and Raven got a sense of warmth and love. Arian walked to the door and waited for someone to let her out. That was when Raven noticed that everyone had started to walk off the women continued to wail from their grief but some of the men had gathered around the cart. They seemed to be waiting for Lady Leena to tell them what to do with the lord's bodies.

Raven noticed that Azure had disappeared she began to look around for him and saw that he was surrounded by his brothers and some of the guards. They seemed to be talking about something. She decided that she would try to walk over to them and hear what was going on. Her body moved slowly at first but quickly found a rhythm, as if her body had always known it was a wolf. Once she was over at the circle, she heard Azure ask Draco if he had felt anything.

"No, and that is what is strange. I stopped paying attention to how Lord Markus's magic felt. Not to mention Lady Arian's that way I would stop think that we were being attacked. All I can think is that someone that shares Raven's and Lord Markus's magic crossed the boundary and I failed to notice it. I am so sorry my brothers please forgive me." Draco said the last part with his head down.

"It is not your fault Draco. I know who attacked our father and Lord Markus. Oryeon, I need you to call a severe storm one that will wash out the roads and keep everything in their dens and all the people in their homes. For a few days. I am going to send out the massagers to all the towns to warn about the storm. I need the storm in two days. Can you, do it? Beo, I need you? talk to the generals and form a plan of attack. With the storm I am hoping that Gaspar will end up being stuck on our land. If I am correct in where he attacked the lords, it is an area that floods around a small piece of land that creates an island. With a severe enough storm, he will be stuck there for weeks. During that time, I am planning on the other clans to join us in seizing his holdings and placing the rightful heir on the throne." Azure spoke with a commanding voice that held a wealth of power.

He turned and looked directly at Raven he grinned just before he turned his attention back to the guards. At that point she decided to go look for her mother. There was still a servant standing by the front door and as Raven approached, he opened it. She was surprised that even though it was totally dark outside she could see the courtyard very well. She saw that over by what had at one time been a flowering garden, her mother sat staring out at the dead flowers. Raven sat down next to her and leaned against into her mother's side. She hadn't realized until that moment how wonderful it felt to just spend quiet time with another person. No matter how long they sat there neither one seemed to notice the cold that was creeping in.

"Lady Raven, Lady Arian, please come in the hour grows late." An unknown masculine voice said from behind them.

Arian got up first and waited for Raven to join her before she walked into the keep. Once they went inside Raven noticed that no one was in the great hall. The wailers were gone as were the bodies, the hall was eerily silent. The two she-wolves walked up the stairs. Arian walked Raven to her room and then turned and walked back down the hall towards what Raven figured was her own room. As Raven was standing there, she began to wonder how she was going to be able to change back into her human form. Let alone open the door. She brought up her paw and began scratching at the door. She heard movement in the room and then the door opened.

"I thought that I heard someone at the door" Azure said with a spark of laughter in his eyes. He stepped aside and with a great flare he swung his left arm and bowed slightly in a welcoming way. She sauntered her way in and sat by the bed looking at him. With what she hoped was a look of desperation she wanted to turn back into a human. She had such a desire to have Azure's arms around her that she actually let out a small whine. He chuckled lightly at her and closed the door.

"Let me guess you have no idea how to change back do you?"

Raven looked at him with her head cocked to the side. He started to laugh full out at her. She wanted to ask him what was so funny instead she ended up whining more at him. He stopped laughing and sat down on the bed looking at her.

"All you need to do is think really hard about being a human again." He explained with minimal laughter coming out in his voice.

She closed her eyes and though about having two legs and two arms a mouth that she could talk with. She worked hard to build the picture in her mind. When she opened her eyes, she was looking down at Azure. She could see in his eyes how proud he was of her. He handed her a sleeping dress to put on.

"I need to talk to you and to do that I need you dressed, or I will get distracted." He said in a somber voice. She took the dress and slide it over her head it felt wonderful against her skin as if it had been made of silk. Raven had never had anything feel so wonderful against her skin. She sat down and he grabbed her hands and turned her so that she was looking at him.

"First I want to thank you for giving me a reason to laugh after the horror of my father's death. I am sure that you are hurting as well. With this attack on the lords your brother has signed his own death warrant. The other clans will come, and it will be war unless he is willing to back down. I highly doubt that he will back down. The other important thing is that with my father gone either I have to step up and take over the clan which if I did that then your clan would not have a leader, or I can turn my clan over to my brothers and then you and I can be in charge of your clan. I know that you grew up not knowing the clan rules. Let me explain a big rule is that if a clan does not have a leader, then the other clans will absorb it and divide it amongst themselves. The reason that it did not happen before now is because your father was in charge. It was assumed that your bastard brother would be the clan leader after he was gone. If he had named, you his heir it would have become common knowledge so you would oversee the clan instead of him. However, your brother wanted to rule so much that he prevented this from happening. No one mated pair can rule more than one clan. I am leaving the choice up to you as too whether we call in the other clans for war and for the ceremony to say goodbye to our fathers or if they will be here just for the ceremony. I do have a feeling that the other clan leaders are going to call for war; Lord Markus was not well loved however Lord Griffin was."

After he was done talking, she realized that she was overwhelmed again by everything that had happened in a short amount of time. Now here she was being told that she had to decide if she wanted to have her brother killed over what he did or not.

"Can I have the night to think about everything and I will tell you what I want to do in the morning?" Raven asked hoping that he would grant her the break long enough to think over everything. Azure let go of her hands and stood up.

"Okay I will leave you for the night so that you can think. And sleep without interruption." His voice seemed sad.

"You know this bed is big enough for two." Raven said with a shy smile as she laid down on the bed.

"That maybe love but I don't want to compromise your virtues or your choices." He replied with a half grin, but his eyes were still sad.

"Fine then you can lay on top of the blankets and hold me that way. Just please don't leave me tonight. I don't think that I will be able to rest or think about anything if I am left on my own." Raven said as she climbed under the blanket.

Azure grinned at her and climbed up on to the bed. Raven lost track of how long it took her to fall asleep. Her last thoughts were of how wonderful it felt being held in Azure's arms.

Chapter 12

She awoke with thoughts of her brother and how he needed to pay for what he did. The clan leaders were rumored to begin arriving the next morning. Raven was happy to see her mother sitting with everyone when they broke their fast. As they were finishing their food there was a loud commotion from the courtyard. Azure rushed to the door. Just as he reached it the large doors were slammed open by a large group of people. Raven was still sitting at the table and looking at a large muscular man with a snow-white beard and flaming red hair that was a little shaggy but not by much. His skin was almost as white as his beard. He was so tall that he towered over everyone around him.

"Where is my daughter!?" He hollered in a loud booming voice.

Raven was surprised to see her mother jump up and run to the large man throwing her arms around him, he was still at least 2 feet taller than her. He had to bend down to encircle her waist. She could feel the love radiation from the two of them. Raven stared at them for a long while not sure if she should go introduce herself or just stay where she was. When they broke apart Raven heard her mother say.

"Hello Father, come met your granddaughter. Don't look at me that way I couldn't come home, you know that was the first place Markus would look for me." Raven heard her say the last part as she pulled him down on to the bench where she had just been sitting. Raven turned her attention to where the rest of his men stood and instead saw that Azure had them seated at the other long tables with his men and he was heading back towards her. When he got back by her Raven asked.

"Who is that man?"

"That is Zee-Da leader of Wolf Blood clan of Heather Craig. He is also your grandfather." Azure said the last part with a smile in his voice.

Raven looked at the man next to her mother. She wanted to go over and say hello, however she wasn't sure what to say to him so instead she quickly finished her food and then rushed up to her room. She knew that she was hiding but she was still coming to terms with everything that had happened in a short span of time. Starting with her leaving Rain Rock and ending with her turning into a wolf. She spent hours pacing back and forth in her room. She would walk from one end of the rug to the other over and over. In her pacing she glanced out the window and saw dark storm clouds on the horizon. She stood and watched as the white dots on the hill began to quickly move towards the base of the hill. She saw people rushing around in the village at the base for the hills beyond the keep sturdy stone walls. The longer she watched the harder the wind blew. At the top of the hills the trees looked to be almost doubled over. Their leaves flying off and creating a colorful cyclone as the wind blew. Raven felt that the weather fit her mental state perfectly.

She knew something had to be done about her brother. However, when she took over for Key-Na she made a promise to use her knowledge for healing not for killing. It was then that she felt the wolf in her mind. She felt it wrap around her soul as if to comfort it. It startled her at first until she realized that it had always been there, she just hadn't noticed it before. Raven stood at the window watching as the storm blew in teetering back and forth, between imprisoning her brother or forcing him into exile.

Raven could tell that Oryeon was bringing the rains that night from how hard the wind blew and how dark the clouds looked. Raven remembered Azure had mentioned that he was going to have his men combing the woods to keep Gasper in hiding while they were eating. As Raven watched out the window, she saw the wind start to pick up again. It was almost comical watching the winds pick up a shirt or something that had been left on the line to dry. It was white in color and the wind spun it like a child's top as it yanked the fabric off the line shooting it into the air.

As she stood there watching the fabric disappear into the clouds. she heard a knock on the door. Raven turned towards the door as her mother stepped in. Upon seeing who it was Raven turned back towards the window to continue to watch the storm. She was afraid of what her mother wanted to know. She was still trying to figure out what to say to her grandfather.

"Raven we need to talk. Azure has told me what your brother has done. In addition, with that, the fact that we are sure that he is the one that killed your father and Lord Griffin. Azure is furious. I truly wish that I had been the one to raise you, but the elders would not have it. I know that Key-Na raised you to respect life but, in this instance, maybe you should allow your brother to pay for his crimes to the fullest extent of the laws." Arian placed her hand on Raven's shoulder and looked out the window at the storm gathering. Raven was surprised that her mother wanted to talk about her decision and not how she was hiding from her grandfather.

"I understand that my brother should pay for his crimes, but I can't seem to bring myself to agree to his death. I was going to talk to Azure about putting Gasper in prison for the rest of his life. The other option is to exile him and any children he has for all time. Is it so wrong to seek a different path other than his destruction?" As Raven asked the question, she turned to her mother absently rubbing her shoulder.

"What is wrong with your shoulder? I have seen you rub it several times and I noticed when you were in your wolf form, you were limping." Arian held a tone of concern in her voice.

"Gaspar bit my shoulder a while ago and it has been bothering me since. Azure said that he cleaned it out and took care of it. I am not sure why it is still bothering me. I was planning on talking to the healer of the clan and find out what he has to say on it." Raven replied

Arian went back to looking out the window, Raven had the feeling that the conversation was done, turned her attention back to the window as well. The two women were standing there looking out the window waiting for the rain to start. The first raindrops fell shortly after they stopped talking. The storm was so fierce that day turned to night. The clouds were black and gray, and the rain obscured any vision because of the force that it was coming down with. The rain beat on the glazed window so hard that Raven was afraid that it would break. She unconsciously stepped back from the window and watched as her mother closed the wooden shutters that had been hidden by the drapes on either side. As Arian was hooking the metal latch thunder boomed so loudly that it shook the keep slightly. Raven in awe felt an overwhelming urge to open the shutters back up and watch nature's fury. As she moved towards the window to open it the lighting flashed so brightly around the stutters that it seems thousands of candles were a light and then just as quickly it was dark again as if someone had blown all the candles out. The wind was howling like it was in pain. In a way the wind's howling matched the pain that everyone at the keep was feeling over the lost of the Clan lords.

"I have to admit that young Oryeon has strong abilities. I have not heard of anyone else that is wolf blood being born having the ability to call rains." Arian softly said as she stood and listened to the storm.

"Mother, is everyone born of the five brothers gifted in some way? What does wolf born mean?" Raven asked inquisitively.

"All used to be many generations ago, not so many anymore. That is why I was so surprised to find four brothers all of them with magic of their own. As for what wolf born means it is a simply way of saying that a child is born of two royal blood lines."

Raven looked at her mother with a confused look on her face. "You mean three brothers, right? Beo has no magic just a gifted mind for strategy." Raven said as she sat in one of the chairs.

"Some would say that him having such a mind at such an early age is magic." Arian responded still standing by the window.

"Do you have magic mother?"

"I do not know of any magic ability I have; however, I think that you have healing magic from what Key-Na told me. She hadn't found anyone that was so talented at healing including herself." Arian said as she sat down across from Raven.

"If only the royal family is gifted, then how did Key-Na have magic?" Raven asked.

"From what she told me, a long time ago an ancestor of her's was a bastard child of one of the royal families. The magic followed down through the line. Skipping generations here and there always granting the person healing abilities however they could not shift into a wolf. She said that it was odd that both her and her son had the ability to heal." Arian answered then fell silent.

From the look on her face Raven figured her mother was lost in thought. She took this chance to get out of the rather comfortable chair and walked over to the window. The wind had died down a bit so she was not so worried that the glass would break. As she opened the shutter a bolt of lightning struck, illuminating the road. She saw a group riding fast for the open gate. They galloped through and before Raven lost sight of them, she saw that at the back was a small looking child. The lightning struck again, and Raven saw the party head towards the front of the keep.

Feeling that her healing would be needed Raven turned and rushed out of the room heading to the great hall. As she reached the top of the stairs, she heard someone bellow for a healer from the great hall. As she glanced over the railing, she noticed that the small child that she had seen out the window was now laying on one of the tables. It looked as if there was blood coming from under the child. Raven saw a bald portly man with a full beard standing next to the table. He was too far away for her to really see his features; she could see his mouth moving but he was too quiet. Raven quicken her pace and hurried down the stairs.

She was unaware that her mother had followed her until she heard her holler from the top of the stairs.

"BRING FRESH WATER HEALING HERBS AND FRESH RAGS FOR LADY RAVEN!" Raven was so glad that her mother was handling the gathering of supplies. The heavy-set man was holding the hand of the child. Now that Raven was next to the table, she saw that it was a young woman. Her cloths were soaking wet the left side of her pants was shredded. Before Raven started to cut away the cloth, she looked at the man and asked.

"What happened? What caused these gashes?"

The heavy-set man looked at her and in a low raspy voice said.

"We were attacked on our way here by a large wolf. I am not sure what color it was; it was soaking wet. My daughter Ruby was riding at the back in case we encountered any hostel force on our way here. Please help her. It is my fault that she is here to begin with, I was uncomfortable leaving her at home."

"I see, well with luck she will survive." Raven said as she grabbed one of the rags that had been placed on the table and began to clean the wounds. She discovered four long jagged gashes in Ruby's leg going from the hip down past the knee. Seeing how bad the damage was Raven put all her concentration into stopping the bleeding. She was convinced that this attack was designed to kill or at least cripple a person. It had severed all the way to the bone in a couple places.

Raven knew she had to start with fixing each vein that had been severed. Once that was done, she focused on the muscles. She went slowly and meticulously making it her personal mission to make it so that Ruby would survive and be able to walk. Raven put all of her focus on getting the bleeding stopped and she began to slowly and meticulously stich up the wounds. She barely registered that Azure was talking to someone close to her. After a while even that background noise faded away. She was so intent on her work that all time seemed to stop. All Raven knew was that she never ran out of thread, bandages, and clean water. Fortunately, the child never woke up or seemed aware of what was happening to her.

Chapter 13

*I*t was well into the evening before Raven stood up straight and decided that Ruby was out of danger. Raven started to look at the child and what she saw, shocked her. The girl looked to no more than ten years old with dark red hair. Her skin was pale, and Raven wasn't sure if it was from the blood loss or if it was her normal coloring. She looked around for the gentleman that Ruby had been traveling with. Raven saw him over by the fireplace sitting on the wide bench, it appeared his head was in his hands from the slump of his shoulders. Raven noticed that no one else was around. She also noticed that at some point a blanket had been found and placed on the table for Ruby to be covered up after Raven was done bandaging her.

Raven covered her and walked over to the gentleman. As she got closer, she could hear slight murmuring coming from the man. Raven figured he was praying; she gently placed her hand on his shoulder and just there waiting for him to finish his prayer. When he was done, he placed his hand on top of hers and looked up to her. Raven noticed that his beard was the same dark red as Ruby's hair. She also saw that he had wrinkles around his worry filled grey eyes, the wrinkles made her think that he enjoyed laughing more than any other emotion.

"Sir I have done all that I could, Ruby is sleeping, and the bleeding has stopped. I would suggest that she be taken to a room and given plenty of rest and food when she wakes up. Can you please tell me what happened to you and your party and why you were caught out in the massive storm? Also, why she was traveling with you she looks to be only 10?" Raven asked the last question with a note of dismay in her voice.

"She is old enough to shift therefore she is old enough to travel with her clan leader." He said as he turned and looked at her. Raven noticed that at some time someone broke his nose and it healed crooked.

"I thought that she was 10 because of her size, I meant no disrespect." Raven said as she sat down next to the gentleman.

"My daughter is 16 she has always been small for her age I fear that she will never be able to find a mate because of her small size. My name is Baron by the way I am the leader of the Wolf Song clan of Singing Willow. As you were helping my daughter your mate Azure told me that you are Markus's only legitimate heir. Azure and I believe that it was your brother who attacked my group, in a poor attempt to dissuade us from joining you in your fight against him. However, when he attacked my only child, he solidified my choice in joining against him. If there is any way that I can help more than just to lend my support, please let me know. As for how we were caught in the storm we ended up leaving our home later than I was planning. My wife Maryann suffered a bad fall, and I was torn between leaving her at home on her own or trying to bring her along. In the end Maryann decided to stay at the keep with much of my clan and most of the guards. The few guard that came with me were my personal guard. If it is needed, I can send for the rest of my clans warriors." By the time that he had finished talking his voice was very raspy again.

"A good thing for that throat is some hot water with a little bit of honey in it. I am sure you could find water and honey in the kitchen. Hopefully one of the kitchen maids will be asleep in there near the fire. I am going to bed I am certain the Ruby will be fine for the night. Try and get some sleep Lord Baron." Raven stood up and headed towards the stairs leaving Lord Baron to his own devices.

She was hoping that Azure was in bed however when she opened the door all that greeted her was a small fire in the hearth and an empty room. The rain still was pounding the window so hard that she could hear it through the wood of the shutters. She was afraid that the rain would break the glass and the wind would break apart the shutter. Thunder continued to boom, and the lighting was bright enough that she was seeing the light come around the shutters still. Knowing that there was no way that she would be able to sleep with the storm raging against the window she closed the door and went back down to the great hall. It was quieter with the lack of windows and the thick wooden door. the stone walls also helped to deaden the booms. She did notice that all the windows in the hall were shuttered, just like the window in her room.

Ruby was no longer laying on the table and no one else seemed to be in the hall. She went over and added a few logs to the dyeing fire. She sat down on the bench and stared into the fire. As she sat, she began absently rub her shoulder, it was throbbing again. While she rubbed it, she began to hear a howling over the storm. It was a deep rich and foreboding sound to the point of sending chills up and down Raven's spine. She involuntarily shuddered at the feeling. She sat there with her back to the door in hopes that it was only the wind. Suddenly the front doors banged open so loudly that she let out a scream. With her back to the door, she had to turn to see what happened. The doorway was a dark hole until a lightning strike lite up the outside. In the doorway stood a giant of a man he looked to be 9 feet tall. His hair was long and plastered to his skull. Raven noticed that he had piercingly vivid green eyes. Then she noticed that he was naked and dripping wet.

Raven didn't get a chance to say anything, because the guards that had been near the main hall had heard her scream. They rushed towards the intruder as he dissolved into a huge fierce black wolf with vivid green eyes just like he had when he was human. He was upon the first guard ripping out his throat before the others even reached him. He was rushing towards Raven knocking the guards out of the way by any means that he could. Raven barely had time to stand and try to run before she was knocked down and felt teeth clamped onto the back of her neck. She decided that the best thing to do was lay still.

As she laid there, she could feel his hot breath fanning her hair and his deep rumbling growl vibrating the back of her neck. To fight against her rising panic, she closed her eyes in doing so she was able to remain still. While she laid there, she heard a very loud growl in front of her. Raven opened her eyes and wanted to heave a sigh of relief. Not 10 feet from her stood Azure in his glorious wolfen form. Raven could see the anger flashing in his eyes directed towards the wolf that had her pined to the floor.

"That large black wolf that is staring at you is my husband. I could be wrong, but I think if you don't let me up soon, he is going to ripe your throat out." Raven whispered the only answer that she received was the wolf biting down tighter. Raven could tell that he had broken the skin because she started to feel liquid running down the side of her neck. She knew the moment that Azure smelled the blood because his wolfen face went from just upset to furious.

Raven saw Azure charged towards the black wolf, leaping over it at the last moment. As he sailed over, he must have clamped on to the wolf most likely by the scruff of its neck. Then using his momentum to carry them both away from her, the big wolf let go as he was jerked away. Raven heard the wolves fighting each other. She quickly placed her hand against the side of her neck where she was feeling the liquid dribbling down. With her other hand she pushed herself up into a sitting position. It took her a couple of minutes to dispel the dizziness that plagued her as she sat up.

She could barely follow the combatants; in their fight they looked to be two black blurs. She heard snarls and growls as well as yips. Every time she heard one of the wolves yelp, she was afraid that it was Azure. It seemed that the fight went on for hours, before the two wolves stopped fighting. Raven was feeling increasingly lightheaded as the fight went on. She could feel a stickiness to her dress, but she was too tired to care. The last thing she saw before she pasted out was Azure and the stranger shifting.

Chapter 14

"What do you mean she has been silver poisoned? How? When?" Raven heard Azure talking it sounded like he was extremely far away.

"It appears that a small silver piece was embedded into her shoulder without her knowledge. As for when I am not sure the muscle and tissue around the area showed signs of healing another wound. Has she been wounded within the last 6 months?" asked a youthful voice

"Yes, her brother bit her in that shoulder, is it possible that the silver became embedded then? If so, how could he have done it without getting silver poisoning himself?" Raven was still having a tough time hearing what was going on. It seemed the louder the voices got the more pain she was in. Before the question was answered she lost consciousness.

Raven became aware of her surroundings slowly, the first thing she noticed was that pain was gone. Then came the pounding of the rain on the windows, the sound was so deafening that Raven couldn't seem to hear anything else. She felt someone holding her hand and singing softly. Raven turned her head and felt the muscles in her neck protest the movement. She must have made a sound because, she heard movement and felt someone sit on the bed.

"Love, what is wrong where do you hurt?" Azure asked with concern laced through his voice.

"My neck and shoulder." Her voice was raspy and quiet, Azure could barely hear her.

"Here, give her some water." Raven recognized her mother's voice.

Raven felt Azure slid his arm around her back and help her sit up enough to drink the water. As she was sitting, she opened her eyes and saw her mother standing near the foot of the bed. She looked over and saw that Azure was sitting on the bed with her.

"How are you feeling Lady Raven?" Asked a cheery youthful voice from by the door. She was so startled that she began to choke on the water. Azure slapped her back gently in hopes of clearing her airway.

"I am sorry for scaring you, it was not my intention. Allow me to introduce myself I am Cor. My mother was Key-Na, and I am blessed that she pasted on her healing ability to me. It has allowed me to find my place in my adopted clan."

As Cor was talking Raven noticed how similar he looked to his mother. He had his mother's vivid green eyes and her high cheekbones. He also had her sharp nose, and full mouth. He did have a jagged scar that ran along the left side of his face but, instead of distracting from his handsomeness it enhanced it. However, that is where the similarity ended where Key-Na's hair was white as snow, Cor's hair was coal black. Cor seemed to be in his prime. Not bent by age like Key-Na was when Raven buried her. He wore a brown shirt and black pants that looked as if they had seen better days.

"So, I might have figured out why your shoulder has been throbbing for a long while. It seems that your brother had a sliver of silver embedded in one of his teeth and when he bit you it detached. As Azure told you before silver is a poison to us, however for some reason it did not kill you. I think I know why. You had never changed before that except when you were very little. But once you changed the silver began to work its poison slowly." When Cor finished talking Raven felt blessed that she hadn't died from the poison. Raven softly asked

"What happened after I passed out, I remember Azure and the other wolf fighting and my neck bleeding."

Azure who had been supporting her as she was sitting up gently set her back down on the mattress and got up to pace. All Raven could do was watch him with her eyes. She was so intent on watching him that she did not notice Cor and Arian leave. He would pace for a bit and then stop run his fingers through his hair look at her and begin to pace again. After about 30 minutes of pacing, he sat down on the bed.

"About time you sat down. You were making my dizzy from all the back and forth." Raven said with a slight laugh in her voice. "Now that you are still, will you please tell me what happened?"

Azure took a deep breath and blew it out before he began to talk.

"That big black wolf was Krystopher the clan leader of Wolf Heart. He had been attacked just before reaching our lands. He says that it was a large wolf and then a group of soldiers. The soldiers were wearing my clan's colors. That is why when he came in, he attacked without any provocation. It took you fainting before he came to his senses. The Wolf Heart clan places women above all else, even their own children at times. Once his mind understood what he had done to you he changed and was begging for forgiveness. He right now is in a self-exile place in the northern tower as his way of paying penance to you. I am hoping that now that you are awake, I will be able to fully talk to him and discover what happened. I already asked all of my guards and soldiers if they did attack, and they swear that they did no such thing."

Azure stood back up and Raven afraid that he would begin to pace again reached for his hand to stop him before he could start.

"Allow me a few days to recover and then you and I both will go and talk to Krystopher. I have another question for you. How is the girl Ruby doing?" She asked in a stronger sounding voice then she had before.

"My mother is with her now; she is healing, and I think that it is helping my mother as well. Come to find out that Leena and Baron are cousins through marriage; they grew up together and were very close. Apparently, my mother left the clan in not so good standing and her and Baron haven't spoken or written each other for several years. She did not know that he had married or that he had a child. I can see that you are getting tired rest now love I will not be far." Azure placed a kiss on Raven's forehead and sat there holding her hand until she fell asleep.

It was several days before Raven was strong enough to be up and about for longer than 30 minutes at a time. Azure helped her walk down to the hall and then over to one of the long benches as she sat down, he asked one of the servants to go and retrieve Krystopher. Raven felt a little apprehension at seeing the giant of man that attacked her. She kept repeating that he didn't know what he was doing, and that Azure was there to protect her.

Raven could hardly recognize the man that walked in behind the servant, he was so thin and haggard looking. He was wearing what looked to be a coarsely woven cloth that was the shape of a tunic. It had no sleeves and reached his knees; it was held in place by a rough piece of rope. Krystopher kept his eyes down cast the whole time that he was walking towards Raven. Once he reached her, he sank to one knee and bent his head as if asking her to decide if he should live or die.

In her most regal voice Raven said, "I understand that you came here right after a fight on my husband clan's lands. I also understand that you attacked feeling that you had just cause. However, you did kill one of our guards and almost me as well." With that comment his shoulders fell even more, and he fell to his other knee.

"Nevertheless, you did not succeed in killing me. You were attacked on our lands, coming to our aid. My decision is that you must compensate the guard's family that you killed in some way. Also, you have to stop your exile we need strong allies against my brother. I forgive you Krystopher, leader of the Wolf Heart clan. Azure and I understand if you would rather not fight alongside us because of what happened on our lands. We will insist that if you don't fight with us that you not fight with Gaspar either."

Krystopher raised his head and looked Raven in the eyes.

"I thank you for your forgiveness. I also accept your terms and I will fight alongside you. As for the guard's family how best do you think that I should compensate them, good Lady Raven?"

Raven thought about it for a couple of minutes and said. "First question is are you truly sorry for killing the guard. The second question is, are you married or have children that rely on you?"

"Yes, I am my Lady. No, my Lady I have no mate and I have no children. Why do you ask, surely you don't expect me to marry this widow?" Krystopher asked in shock.

"No nothing like that good sir. After we take care of my brother Gasper, I would ask that you help the widow and her children for 6 months. At the end of that time, you can choose to continue to help the family or leave and go back to your clan. Do you accept these terms?" Raven responded.

"Yes, I accept those terms." He said with his head held high

"Good. Please get something to eat so that you may regain your strength. Also find some more befitting cloths." As Raven said the last part, she signaled one of the servants over. "Please take Krystopher to the kitchen and help him get something to eat. As well as some cloths"

"Food sounds like a wonderful idea. Lady Wife how about we go to the kitchen as well and get something to eat." Azure asked as he held his hand out for Raven. She placed her hand in his and allowed him to help her up. They headed hand in hand into the kitchen. Once there they found some fresh bread as well as a couple apples. After gathering up the food, the two of them headed back into the main hall and sat for a while enjoying each other's company.

Chapter 15

Several days later all the clan leaders were in the great hall sitting around two tables that had been pushed together to form one large table. It was still raining but not as hard as it had been. Gaspar was not found, and Azure had agreed to give up the hunt for him. The leaders were discussing the best way to assault Rose Hedge and get revenge for the murder of Lord Markus and Lord Griffin. Raven sat and listened to all the leaders talk and argue about the best way to attack Gaspar. As she sat there listening, she heard laughter coming from behind her. She turned around and saw Ruby and Draco chasing each other. Ruby was limping slightly and had a stick with colorful ribbons on the top of it. The ribbons fluttered in the air as she ran around Draco. He kept reaching for her and Ruby would dance right out of his reach again and again. Raven was struck with an idea for how to storm the manor.

"Let's have a parade in Rose Hedge." She said with a giggle to the clan leaders.

"What do you mean have a parade?" Zee-Da asked in confusion as he turned to face her.

"You mean after the battle, right?" Baron asked in a confounded voice.

Krystopher just looked at her and so did Azure. They both wore a look of curiosity.

"No, I mean have a parade right up to the manor door. No one will think anything of it, especially if we all wear disguises. For example, if you all saw a group of people in colorful garments and brightly colored masks. With ribbons and drums and laughter would you think you were being attacked or would you think it was traveling show for entertainment?" She asked the leaders.

Azure grinned and said "No, I would welcome them into my home to entertain me and any guests that I had."

"As would I," responded Zee-Da.

"I think anyone would because, no one thinks anything of a traveling group. In fact, most of the time I know a head of time that they will be coming through. So, I make sure that I have a feast ready for them." replied Krystopher.

Before anyone else could say anything, a loud squeal resounded throughout the hall followed by a lot of laughing. Everyone looked to where the sound came from and saw that Draco had finally captured Ruby and both of them were laughing as only children could.

"That is it. That is how we will do it. I have to say that I have a wonderful wife and a smart one at that." Azure said his face beaming. Raven blushed and bowed her head at the compliment.

After the decision was made that the carnival would be held in two months just in time for the last harvest of the year. Then the leaders focused on how best to sneak weapons into Rose Hedge, and how many men they would have. Also, messengers were to be sent to nearby villages with a message for all seamstresses to come to the keep. As the meeting went on Raven would point out certain things that needed to be addressed, such as how they would have to have women in the group as well or else it would be hard to convince people that they were truly a traveling group. Also, children but only those that knew how to either run and hide if in danger or knew how to properly handle a knife. By the time that supper was ready to serve the leaders had a good plan in place. As the food was place on the table Cor approached Raven, she stood up and met him halfway.

"How are you fairing today my Lady? Any pain or other problem?"

"I am tired, and my shoulder still pains me if I move it too much but, other than that thank you Cor for asking" Raven replied

"Your name is Cor?" Krystopher asked coming up behind Raven his voice laced with curiosity.

"Yes, it is my lord. Is there something I can do for you?" he replied in a confident voice.

"Tell me how did you come by this name. What clan are you from?" he demanded rather gruffly. As he stepped aggressively toward Cor.

Cor stepped up and tried to moved Raven behind him as if to shield her from Krystopher. Instead she stayed firmly by his side. Cor responded in a calm voice.

"My mother named me after an ancestor. The same one that had a bastard child with a servant girl and then forced them to leave. The only thing that my family was granted from his noble line was our ability to heal others. That my lord is where I get my name and that is why I don't have a clan." Cor spoke the last sentence with a snarl to his voice. By the time Cor had finished talking Krystopher's face was as white as snow. Raven was looking back and forth between the two of them in confusion.

"I apologize for my behavior my lord; I am very touchy about my ancestry. My mother was always proud of the fact that we had noble blood. I on the other hand am always upset by the fact that I cannot claim a clan for my own. Please do not get me wrong Lady Raven; I greatly appreciate your husband's clan taking me in. Also, your clan for allowing my mother to live there. But I will always ach for my own clan by blood." Cor said the last with so much sadness in his voice Raven was almost in tears. Cor walked over to the bench sat down.

Krystopher and Raven sat down and looked at Cor, he glanced at both and heaved a great sigh. Azure came over to where the three of them were sitting and laying a hand on Cor shoulder said,

"You will always have a home here with my clan."

"I know that, and I truly appreciate that Lord Azure, I am sorry for my outburst Lord Krystopher. My life has not been an easy one. Feeling lost even when I am surrounded by people I care for and trust is hard." He said the last with no emotion in his voice, but Raven knew exactly how he felt.

"That is not required Lord Azure, Cor is part of my clan. I believe he is descended from my great grandfather. He had strong healing abilities and he always was chasing after anything in a skirt. It was assumed all his bastards died in their infancy. The reason was because a witch had cursed him for getting her only daughter with child. All would have been fine except that both the girl and the child died in childbirth. The very day after their deaths the woman walked into the keep with a dagger. She walked up my great grandfather sliced his cheek open and as he bled, she stabbed herself in the stomach with the same dagger. As she lay dying on the stones she shouted. "All of your seed shall wither and died. If not from your lady wife only death, will you find one day from birth!" Of course, no one believed the woman until the babes started dying. It was several years later that his second wife finally gave birth to a son. Before you ask his first wife was killed by thieves when she was on her way to visit a neighboring clan. I must ask do you know the name of your grandmother?"

Raven noticed the look of pure shock on Cor's face. It took Cor a few minutes to answer Krystopher. When he finally did, he said that he did not know her name. All his mother and her mother before her ever said was that they should be proud of their heritage.

"I suggest that you finish your conversation after we eat." Raven said as she grabbed Azure's hand and walked over to where servants were laying out plate after plate of food. She heard benches being moved around the hall so that everyone had a place to sit and eat at the tables. Raven watched from her seat as the large meeting table was separated back out in to two tables and benches were moved for more seating. Supper was a quiet event and as soon as it was over, Cor and Krystopher walked over to the small table that had been placed over in a corner so people could visit, she guessed that they were going to continue their conversation. Raven finished eating and Azure grabbed her hand. He stood up and tugged on it slightly to encourage her to stand up. Once there were standing, he led her up the stairs and into their room.

"Tonight, you are all mine wife. No interruption." He said in a husky voice as he closed the door

"Yes, husband. No interruptions." She said as she backed up towards the bed. When she felt the footrest hit the back of her legs she stopped.

Azure approached Raven with a fire in his eye that she had never seen before. Once he reached her, he placed his hands gentle upon her arms he pulled her in for a loving embrace. She could taste the passion from his kiss. As it ignited her body in flames. He gently laid her on the bed all the while kissing her. As she lay there, he glided his hands down her body as if he was savoring every curve.

Shortly after his exploring began, a persistent knocking began on the door. They could not tell who was knocking or how many there were because they could not hear over the pounding of their own enflamed blood. The knocking came repeatedly finally with a fierce growl of annoyance, Azure got up and stomped over to the door. When he threw open the door there stood a servant girl from what Raven could see she was trembling and crying. Raven could hear Azure's low growl as he stood there waiting for the girl to speak.

When she finally was able to speak her voice trembled "Please, please, I know that you are not to be interrupted. But I could not find Cor anywhere, no one can. My mother is about to give birth and she has been having a difficult time with this pregnancy." She began to cry again.

"Please, please I need Lady Raven's help. My mother needs her help."

Seeing the young woman standing there crying a pleading almost broke Raven's heart. She got up and walked to her husband.

"We will finish this another time love. Someone needs my help, and I cannot turn them away." Raven said as she placed her hand on his chest right over his heart. Azure looked into her eyes and Raven saw concern and compassion

"You go tend to her mother I will find Cor."

Raven kissed him, letting him silently know that she was as passionate as he was. As well as still on fire from their earlier kisses. Before it became too much, she broke it off and followed the young woman. Raven followed the young woman out of the keep, glad that it was a full moon. She was able to easily follow the young woman to a cottage not far from the keep.

"What is your name?"

"It is Eve." As the women got closer Raven could hear someone screaming, Eve and her broke out in a run. The woman on the bed looked very warn and ill by the fire light when Raven stepped into the cottage. A foul stench assaulted her nose and made her stomach roll in protest of it.

"Eve open the door and let this stench out. When you are done with that go to the keep and get my mother. Ask her to bring lavender and sage bundles to help with this smell. Move quickly now." Raven said in a voice that rang with authority and urgency.

Eve hastened to do what was asked of her. Raven went to the pump that she saw by the front of the house. It took several trips between the house and the pump to fill the pot that she placed over fire. By the time that she was done her mother had shown up and was hanging the herb bundles from the rafters. The smell had dissipated enough for Raven to be able to breathe easier, and she was sure that the woman was as well.

It was several hours later before Eve had a new baby brother. Raven told Eve to keep her mother in bed for two weeks so she could heal. Arian and Raven walked back to the keep. Both very tired. After making sure her mother reached her room Raven continued to hers. Not have the energy to undress, she crawled on to an empty bed and was asleep before her head hit the pillow.

The next morning Raven awoke alone in bed, but someone had changed her cloths and placed her under the blankets sometime during the night. At the morning meal Cor and Krystopher came in. Raven watched Azure stormed over to Cor and in a very loud voice demanded to know where he had gone the night before, and that someone had needed his help the night before. The hall was so quiet you could hear a needle drop. Raven watched Cor as he hung his head in shame and told him that he and Krystopher had gone for a long walk. Before Azure could say anything else Krystopher stepped in front of Cor and said.

"It is not my cousin's fault. I am the one to blame I was curious as to his family line. In truth he is my great-grandfather's first wife's great grandson. His mother was told a lie by her mother no doubt thought up to protect them. If you have need to be angry, be angry at me." Krystopher responded in a very curt tone. Azure just nodded his head and walked back over to the table and sat down next to Raven. Raven noticed that Cor walked with more confidence than he had before.

Once Krystopher and Cor were at the table Krystopher announced that Cor was of royal blood. Everyone was stunned for a moment, and then the hall erupted into congratulations. The rest of the morning was spent finishing out the attack plan. It was decided that they would have it as a harvest carnival. Brightly painted gourds, bright autumn colored clothing, everything focused on the harvest. It was also decided which women and children should be allowed to go into battle and what weapons could be smuggled in. After the midday meal the men went outside to begin to construct the wagons that would house the weapons and a safe place for anyone not fighting to hide.

The first seamstress showed up that night before supper. Raven had Azure convert one of the large rooms in the keep into a sewing room. Raven supervised moving the looms from the village into the keep and then into the work room so everything could be in one place. There were looms all over the room so that way several bolts of fabric could be being worked on at the same time. Large wooden tubs had been placed in the courtyard, for easy of dying the fabrics.

It was two weeks before all the seamstresses in the area were at the keep working. Because there were so many of them, they had to do two shifts, one shift was working during the day and the other was working at night. Raven helped during the day whether it was weaving the fabric or dying the cloth. She hardly ever saw her mother or Azure's mother, however when she did, the ladies were always together. It was very rare when she saw one and not the other.

When she could, she would check on the young guard and was pleased to see that he was not suffering any ill effects from his attack. He told her that because he could not hold a sword well, he became a sentry and kept a lookout on the wall. He also told Raven how his sister was placed in the kitchen as the servant, who took food out to the sentries, she seemed very happy in that position. Raven even saw Eve's mother; she helped the seamstresses to dye the cloth as Eve watched all the young children. At the end of every day Raven was so tired that she practically fell into bed, falling asleep before her head even hit the pillow. It took a month before everything was ready for the attack on Rose Hedge keep.

Chapter 16

At the end of the month all the unwed and un-engaged women were gathered in the courtyard after the cloth was done being dyed cut and sewn into costumes. The clan lords asked each of them if they knew how to dance or were good at singing. Or if any of them knew how to fight with a sword or a bow. Several of the women could sing and dance. However, they had no desire to learn how to fight. 19 of the women had talents in dancing and singing and had an interest in learning how to fight. The clan leaders agreed that 19 would be passable amount for a carnival.

Each clan lord took charge of 4 of the women. Raven was with Azure, and it was not long before she discovered that she had a natural talent for the bow. She felt that it was her duty to stand beside her husband and avenge her father. Even though she was married, it was something that she felt such conviction for that Azure did not even try to talk her out of it. Then one night Arian came up to her after dinner and handed Raven her cloak.

"Come walk with me daughter, we need to talk." The two of them walked out into the crisp night air.

"Have you tried to shift since your father's passing?" Raven looked down at the ground and sheepishly said "It hurt so much the first time that I have been afraid to try since.

"I understand that baby," she said lifting Raven's head up. "However, you were forced to change out of pain. When you change from not pain or fear. It feels different, and the more often you change the quicker and less painful it becomes."

"How do I change mother? I have been meaning to ask Azure about it but every time I start to ask, something comes up."

"You reach for the change. Think of the wolf her strength, her knowledge and her speed. I would warn you that, if possible, always call the change when you are in a safe and private place. Without the hindrance of cloths, your wolf will not panic because she feels trapped. When you are ready to walk on two legs reach for that change. However, I would advise that you change back in privacy as not to be embarrassed."

"Would you be willing to come with me to my room and help me each night after practice?"

"Of course, I will." Arian said before they headed back inside.

It took two weeks for everyone to be trained most of the women showed great skill with bows a small handful were comfortable enough to use swords. After the weapons training and the shifting, Raven went to bed sore and tired every night. Azure never pushed for his marital rights and Raven was thankful for his restraint, he would simply help her undress and then brush out her hair then they would both go to sleep. Two days before they were to leave for the attack, it snowed heavily. It was too early in the year for the snow to stick around. The Lords worried about their lands and clans with the early snow fall decided to depart with the promise to return in a week, two weeks at the latest. The following day while everyone was making ready to leave for their homes Lord Baron said.

"Lord Azure, I must apologize that Ruby and I must leave on the marrow, I have to get back to my wife. I will send my guards back once Ruby and myself are home safe. I am not sure how my wife is fairing, and I cannot state for sure that I will be able to join you on your mission." Raven watched as Draco looked at Ruby with a scared look on his face.

"No, Ruby you can't leave!" He said jumping up from the table. Before anyone said anything else Azure stood up and said.

"If it pleases you, Lord Baron please accept my youngest brother Draco, into your service to be trained by your master of the guards. He could use a change of scenery and I believe that he is quite smitten with your Ruby." Raven saw that Azure had a large grin on his face when he said the last bit.

Lord Baron stood up with a grin as well and agreed to watch over Draco, he reached over the table and clasped Azure's hand. Draco about jumped over the table in his rush to hug Ruby. Before anything else could be said the cook came rushing into the great hall, with a stricken look on her portly face.

"I have grievous news Lord and Lady. The honey was left out in the yard by one of the serving boys and now it is thick, and it will not work for the Honey Cooked Pears that I was planning on cooking for this evening.

"Why not set it by the fire to warm up so that it can be used?" Raven asked she knew that Key-Na would do that in the winter when the honey was a solid mass.

"I would my lady, if I could, however Krystopher and Cor killed a boar earlier today. I have already cleaned it and prepared it to cook overnight and serving it tomorrow midday. If I were to put the honey by the fire, I am worried that the grease from the boar would get into the honey and change the flavor. Also possibly making it flammable." Upon hear that Raven had an idea spark in her head.

"What would happen if you were to mix grease, honey, and flour?" she asked to no one particular. The cook tugged on her short gray hair with a concerned look on her face and replied.

"The grease would turn the flour and honey into a paste, and it would all taste like fat. It would also mold rather quickly, I would imagine. Why do you ask my lady"?

"Good. Madam cook please don't worry about the dessert tonight instead set all of the kitchen helpers to collect as much of the Boar grease as they can safely. I am going to be trying an experiment tomorrow."

Raven glanced at Azure and saw the most confused look on his face. She began laughing at his perplexed look.

"I would like to see this experiment Lady Raven" said Lord Baron

"You shall, I am hoping that it will help in our fight against my brother."

The rest of the day and into the evening was spent honing fighting skills as well and double checking all the wagons and doing any alteration needed to the costumes. Raven hardly saw Azure throughout the day, when she did see him, he seemed distracted and in a rush.

After a long day Raven was eagerly looking forward to her bed. Instead upon reaching her room and opening the door she was greeted by Azure pulling her into a forceful hug lifting her off the floor.

"I am so proud of you wife. I have a surprise for you." He said as he spun her around a couple of times, causing Raven to laugh from the joy of it.

"Close your eyes and trust me." Raven could tell that he was up to something, she saw the glint of mischief in his hazel eyes.

She looked at him with what she hoped was a shrewd look on her face, but she could not stop the giggle of joy that worked its way out of her mouth. She closed her eyes and felt him turn her around, not knowing if she could open her eyes, yet she kept them closed. She felt him lift her braided hair over her shoulder and untie the back of her dress. She went to turn around and he placed his hands on her shoulder and told her to stay still. She huffed out her breath in annoyance but did as she was asked. She felt Azure push her dress and under dress down off her shoulders and down her arms. It was an interesting sensation to Raven to feel the fabric slide against her skin but not to see it. By the time she felt the dress puddle on the floor at her feet she realized that she was standing completely naked. Before she could try and cover herself, she was suddenly whooshed off feet and out of pure instinct she wrapped her arms around Azure's neck. She felt and heard him laugh at her reaction.

"Easy love. I have you." His voice was soft and comforting, she still had her eyes closed when he bent down and placed her into a hot bath. She was so surprised that her eyes popped open. She was in the largest wooden tub she had ever seen. The tub was lined with copper and the water had a sweet smell to it. She could stretch out in the water and be completely covered with the water. She watched as Azure pulled a stool over and disappeared behind her head. She felt him grab her thick braid and slowly unbraid it. She looked around and saw that fireplace was lit and that a bear skin rug had been laid in front of it.

"This feels amazing my love. How did you think of it?" She heard him chuckle softly and he said.

"It was your mother's idea. She mentioned how hard you have been working on shifting and practicing with the weapons." He said as he brushed out her hair.

"I never did get my question answered, you know the one about how you healed my mother. If I remember correctly Gasper attacked us before you could answer me." She said as she let the hot water relax every sore muscle in her body.

"Huh, you're right I never did. I guess things just kept coming up. So, what I did for your mother it takes a lot of energy so I don't do if I can help it. I can speed up time in a small area. So it was easy to speed up the healing of the gash on Arian's side than speed up your healing. I did try however I realized that if we were both out cold, we would be unprotected. I had a feeling that the grey wolf was Gasper, but I wasn't positive. If I had killed him that night instead of stopping myself things would be better, but I was so concerned about you seeing me in that form that I stopped myself." Raven heard the sorrow in Azure's voice as he admitted his choice. She turned around in the tub to look at him she felt a slight tug on her hair as it flowed through Azure's fingers. She reached both her hands to him as she knelt in the tub. He clasped her two smaller hands in him large rough hand. Raven saw sorrow and love mixed in his eyes and upon seeing his turmoil she placed a hand on his cheek.

"My love, at that time I did not know that I loved you. I did not know that you were the home place that I was longing to find. I don't know if I would have run from you at seeing you change or if I would have stayed. I regret somethings that happened. However, I am so glad for so much more than I regret. Now leave me to my soak my love, the fire needs more wood why don't you go and get some." She said as she grinned and patted his cheek at the last part. He chuckled and stood up, once he was standing, she turned and went back to relaxing in the tub. She heard him open the door and close it behind him.

She leaned her head back in the tub making sure to drape her hair outside of it to keep it dry. She closed her eyes enjoying the heat of the water she felt herself become drowsy and fell asleep.

Chapter 17

The day of the attack dawned brightly; they had camped the carnival in the meadow the day before. Everything was in good order; the weapons were sharp the costumes bright and colorful. As Raven looked out the house window it looked as if the meadow was a flutter with thousands of autumn leaves. The few children that had come knew that once the fighting started, they were to hide in the wagon. The dancers that were trained to use swords had them hidden within the many folds of their skirts. It weighed heavy on Raven's hearts that some lives on both sides would be lost today. Before her musings could drag her into a pit of anguish, she felt Azure's arms circle her waist.

"You are frowning my love. We have planed and prepared for this day, I truly hope that no ones dies however, I cannot promise. Now come away from the window and get into your costume. We need to get moving sooner rather than later." Azure said as he turned her away from the window and guided her over to where her costume laid on the bed. It took no time with Azure's help for Raven to change cloths and be ready to head into town. She lifted her half mask and had Azure tie it on for her. The adults all had half masks to hide who they really were in hopes of not being noticed. All the masks were brightly painted in yellows and reds some of the dancer's masks had feathers, Raven was very glad that her mask didn't have any.

The group left the meadow with pipes playing a lively tune and drums keep time. They wanted to be heard long before they were seen. The children ran ahead of the group with instructions to tell everyone about the carnival. Just as before they reached town about mid-day their plan had worked the people of the village were out in the street eager to see the performers. Azure afraid that someone would notice Raven, suggested that she drive the wagon at the back keeping her head down. They made their way trough town and headed to the keep as if they had been expected. Even from the back she could see that the portcullis was down. The plan had been to just walk right up to the front door, so this was unexpected. Everyone stopped playing and the children quieted down it was so quiet that Raven was sure they had been found out.

"HAIL TO THE HOUSE IS THE LORD HOME?" Raven recognized Lord Baron's voice he wasn't shouting in anger he just seemed to project his voice. Raven couldn't hear the response then Lord Baron was speaking again.

"HAIL AND GOOD HEALTH TO YOU SIR. WE ARE THE TRAVELING CARNIVAL KNOWN AS LAST FEAST. WE HAVE COME HERE IN HOPES OF ENTIERTAINING THE NEW LORD OF ROSE HEDGE." There was a pause and then Lord Baron responded

"YES, WE HAVE DANCERS AND A FORTUNE TELLER ALONG WITH TRICKS AND MUSICIANS GALOR. WE HOPE TO PROVIDE A BIT OF AUTUMN FUN BEFORE WINTER." Another pause then a loud cheer as Raven heard the portcullis squeal loudly as it was raised. Now she began to hold her breath this was the most nerve grating part of the whole plan. They formed a semi-circle around the entrance she made sure to keep her head down and stayed towards the back of the group as they walk into the main hall. The kids began running around and creating a wonderful distraction for the guards. Raven was surprised at what she saw, the once beautiful stones had scorch marks on them. The vines and roses were burnt to cinders she looked around and saw the once blood red flag had been replaced by a black flag. Where when she had first seen the keep, she had been in awe of the beauty, now she felt a sinister heaviness to it. The fear in the air seemed almost physical.

The guards seemed almost eager to open the hall doors. Everyone walked in, she was the last in the door. As soon as she was inside the doors slammed shut plunging the world into darkness momentarily. Before Raven's eye could adjust, she heard a voice that made her skin crawl.

"Who are you all?" Raven glanced around her the voice seemed to come from everywhere and nowhere at the same. As she glanced around, she saw that her brother was sitting on a high-backed chair in the middle of the room. It was very easy to see him, he sat up on a dais with candelabrum on either side. She saw that a serving girl was being held on his lap against her will. Raven could see Gasper's fingers digging into the poor girl's neck.

"Gasper under wolf law I challenge you for right to rule the Wolf Tear Clan. You are a usurper and have no legal claim to the throne. Before you killed Lord Markus, he named his first-born Raven his successor." Raven watched as Azure stepped up on the first step of the dais.

"Who are you to challenge me for my clan?" It sounded like Gasper growled his question more than asked it.

"I am Azure, eldest son of Lord Griffin leader of the Wolf Soul clan." Azure stepped up one more step he was almost face to face with Gasper. Raven's heart was in her throat watching Azure be that close Gasper. Raven heard the girl whimper and then her brother snarl at the girl as he threw her off the dais. Raven watched as Lord Baron tried to catch the girl. Then she heard a deafening growl that reverberated around the hall she turn just in time to see Gasper and Azure tumble from the dais. She heard growls and flesh hitting flesh she could not get close enough to see what was happening. The combatants were in the middle of the ring of performers, every time she tried to get close to the inside someone would push her to the outside of the ring.

Then it happened, she felt a rendering of her soul dropping to her knees in pain and anguish. A howl sounded, she looked up and saw her brother's rage filled eyes staring at her as he sliced his claws across her throat. She fell forwards and saw Azure's decapitated body, his head nowhere to be seen. Her world darkened as she felt her blood pool under her body, she knew that there was no way she would survive. She died with a howl locked in her throat unable to give it voice.

Chapter 18

Raven awoke howling she was still in her tub the water had cooled. The door slammed open Raven screamed and looked over her shoulder. Azure was rushing into the room a look of sheer predator on his face.

"What is Raven? What has happened?"

"Nothing my love. A horrible dream. It felt so real." Raven could feel the tears streaming down her face. She was unsure if they were from the realism of the dream or if they were from sheer relief that it was not real. She drew her knees up to her chest and wrapped her arms tightly around them.

"Oh, my love it was only a dream. Here let's get you out of the water and warming up by the fire. I dropped the wood in the hall when I heard you howl. I will go get it and then I will help you out of there." He said as he stood up. Raven nodded her head and continued hugging her knees. She had no idea how long it took for Azure to return and help her out of the tub. He wrapped her in a blanket and had her sit in front of the fire.

Raven seemed to watch what was happening to her from a distance, almost as if she was still in a dream. She watched as Azure listened to her dream and once done, he knelt down on the floor in front of her. Feeling him wrap his arms around her waist brought her back to herself, she felt him placed his head in her lap. She leaned over him and rubbed his back in small circles. Raven was not sure how long they stayed there just holding each other. It was Azure that moved first sitting back on his heels.

"Come love it is time for sleep. I will keep the terrors away." He stood up and reached his hand down to her. She placed her hand in his and let him pull her out of the chair. He guided her over to the bed. She moved the blankets and crawled in between them, she felt the bed dip under Azure's weight. He pulled the blankets up around her and snuggled against her back.

The next morning Raven awoke to discover that Azure had again awaken before her. She was still shaken a bit from the dream the night before. She dressed making sure to take her time as a way to calm her nerves. She headed to the main hall to break her fast she was pleasantly surprised to see Krystopher breaking his. She smiled at him and descended the stairs by the time she was sitting she had a plate with some bread and cheese on it sitting in front of her on the table.

"Krystopher what does wolf law mean when calling for a challenge?"

"Um…good morning to you as well Lady Raven. Has someone dared challenge you?" He looked about the hall as if looking for the fool that would challenge her. Before she could answer there was a scream from the kitchen, Raven still thinking about the dream stood up and rushed to the door before she had a chance to think about what she was doing. Krystopher was a slightly faster and opened the door before she could. Raven had a split second to see what was happening, before Krystopher doubled over from a mud splattered child hitting him in the stomach. It was so forceful that both the child and Krystopher fell backwards onto the stone floor outside the kitchen.

"Tomas are you alright?" Asked a breathless girl's voice. Raven looked back into the kitchen where the voice had come from. She looked and saw two young girls about 10 years old standing in the doorway to the garden covered in mud almost as much as the other child. One girl was wearing a worn blue dress and the other's dress was just as worn but, it was green. They both had red hair and looked very similar however their eye color was different. One's eyes were as green as springtime ferns and the others was as blue as a clear blue summer sky. The girl in the blue dress slowly walked the rest of the way across the kitchen as if to grab the child out of Krystopher's arms. As the girl in the blue dress walked over the other one said from the doorway.

"I must apologize for my brother, we were supposed to be helping bring in the last of the food in the garden, when Tomas found a mud puddle to play in, he is only 6 and gets distracted easily. My sister Beth and I, my name is Mary by the way. Tomas decided that we needed a mud bath so, he began throwing the mud at us. My sister and I not wanting to be seen as weak attached him with mud as well. He screamed when we pushed him down in the mud." She finished with a sheepish look. As she had talked, she walked across the kitchen by the time she was done all three children were standing in front of Krystopher and Raven. Krystopher was kneeling still trying to wipe the mud off Tomas's face. Raven saw that the boy had the same red hair as his sister's she couldn't see his eyes because, he was looking at Krystopher.

"Okay, Mary. Who is your mother, and father?" Raven asked.

"My mother's name is Nara she is one of the bakers in the keep. My Father was killed not that long ago here at the keep." Mary had a tear running down her face as she said the last part.

Raven could see Krystopher's face it looked like he had just been punched in the stomach again at hearing what she said. Raven could see his guilt came rushing to the surface because she knew that the only guard that had been killed recently had been the one, he killed. He gently reached out and grabbed Mary's shoulders.

"Where could we find your mother now?" He asked very gently and smiled at her as if she was the only person in the whole world. Raven saw that cheered her up,

"Since she is not in the kitchen then she maybe over at Cor's house. She brings him bread and other sweets when she bakes too much."

Krystopher stood up and looked at the children with a concerned look on his face. Raven knew that it was at least an hour walk to Cor's house.

"Do you have cloaks for the walk?" Raven asked

"No, my Lady, they were ruined last winter. Mother and Father were going to have new ones made for us but, then he was killed, and mother became distant." Beth responded. Raven could tell that the continued talking of the children's father was causing the children to become more upset.

"How about we go and see if we can find some fabric and make you three unique cloaks." She asked as she reached out her hand to each of the girl's.

The children's faces lite up at the thought of having something different, that was when she saw that Tomas's eyes were the color of springtime oak leaves. Krystopher followed Raven and the children to the sewing room. Over in the corner was a large box full of scrapes from the costumes that had been made. While the children were squealing in joy at all the bright colors, Krystopher excused himself signaled for Raven to step over to the side with him.

"I feel so horrible about what has happened. How do I fix this dear Lady?" He asked with tears in his eyes. He looked so lost right at that moment that all Raven could do was give him a hug. As she was releasing him, a woman came running full tilt into the room. She had copper red and vivid blue eyes she was rather tall.

"Have you seen my children?" She asked rather franticly and breathlessly Raven recognized her as the baker that made the honey cakes that Raven had fallen in love with.

"Yes, they are in there making new cloaks for winter." Raven said. As she walked out of the room, she saw Krystopher and Nara start talking. Seeing everything in hand she closed the door.

It was afternoon before Raven was able to go out and do her experiment. Her plan was to use the honey, grease and flour mixture in gourds against Gasper's keep's wall as a way for the walls to catch fire. She had everything set up for her experiment. A guard was standing by with a flaming arrow as Raven threw the gourd on the ground. It broke open and spilled all the contents on the ground. The guard lit the arrow and fired, the arrow hit and sputtered out. She was so embarrassed that she turned to run into the keep. She didn't get very far because Azure reached out and grabbed her.

"Shh, it is okay love. It was a thought, now thinking about it my father told me of a hot burning mixture. Much like your idea however it is made of pitch and resin, I can't remember the last ingredient. Lord Baron, do you know the last ingredient?" Azure asked over Raven's shoulder she did not even know that Lord Baron had watched her failure.

"Yes, it is tar. Lady Raven you had a great idea by using the gourds we can brightly paint them and hang them on the wagons. There is a tar pit on the boarder of your area and mine. It will take about 4 days to get there and a couple of days to gather enough tar to really cause damage to Gasper's keep."

"Okay we will leave today for the area if you would be so kind as to come with me Lord Baron. I know that you and Ruby had planned to leave today however if you could postpone your return trip home it would be appreciated. Ruby will be safe here with Raven and Krystopher not to mention my younger brothers."

"Very well. I did receive a message last night saying that my wife was feeling better. I think that our return home can wait until after the attack. The other chiefs should be back shortly after we return."

Azure and Baron left two hours later with a group 30 guards made up from both Lord Baron's and Azures best guards and a wagon full of empty barrels. The men were gone 12 days, it was the longest 12 days of Raven's life. Even when she was on her own looking for a new home she never felt as alone as she did when he was gone. She was not allowed out of the keep per his orders. Her days were spent with her mother, learning all she could about her family history. She also listened to stories that her mother told of the happy times between her and Markus. They also talked about how difficult it was watching Raven grown up without her. Raven would tell her mother stories from her childhood. The only time that she saw any of Azure's family was at meals and sometimes in the evening. Draco and Ruby were always together, Oryeon and Beo would play chess sometimes. However, more often than not as soon as they were done eating, they were back working with the guards, learning how to better use a sword and bow.

The night that Azure came back it was pitch black the stars barely were able to be seen. The wind would gust violently and then settle again as if the gust had not happened. Raven was in the great hall talking with Krystopher who had been absent a lot from the keep the few days. When she asked him where he was spending his day, he told her. If he was not with his cousin Cor, then he was spending time with Nara and her children. Krystopher and Raven were playing a game of chess. Everyone else had gone to bed for the night.

The great hall's door was flung open from a large gust of wind. Krystopher was on his feet and spinning towards the door before it hit the hall's wall. Raven was on her feet quickly, ready to change if she needed to. When she saw that it was Azure standing in the doorway, she rushed to him. The guards and Lord Baron filed in right behind Azure, but Raven barely even notice them. Azure was so tired that he barely kissed Raven before he was leaning on her and heading towards the stairs. She could feel how tired he was his body against hers felt to be made of stone it was so heavy.

She helped him up to their room and into bed. He was snoring lightly before his head even hit the pillow. Wanting to know what happened on their journey, she headed back downstairs. Before she reached the bottom step, she heard many more snores. She saw the guards that had gone with Azure passed out sitting against the wall a couple of them were sleeping against each other's back too tired to find their beds in the barracks. As she did a quick count in her head, she realized that half the men were gone. She saw Lord Baron was sitting at the table a mug of mulled cider in his hand, he looked haggard and worn.

"Please tell us what happened. Why does everyone look as if they haven't slept in a week?" Raven asked as she sat down across the table from Lord Baron.

"I hate to admit this, but your brother is insane. We had no difficulties making it to the tar pit. We had all the barrels filled and loaded up in a very short amount of time. Lord Azure was looking forward to getting home early. Gaspar attacked that night with a small troop of this soldiers. They came out of nowhere. The guards we had on watch were dead before they could utter a sound their throats ripped out. Your brother, in wolfen form, went straight for Azure. your husband barely had time to pull his sword for protection. He struck your brother along the side drawing blood; Gasper ran out of the tent and sent a blood chilling howl as he ran. His soldiers stopped and retreated quickly. They followed us from that time until just outside the keep walls. We could hear his soldiers following us during the day. At night he would come into camp sometimes killing the sentries on duty, sometimes not. We would find his tracks the next morning. Azure and I pushed ourselves and our forces as much as we could every day, but the wagon was loaded down from the weight of the barrels and often became stuck in the mud. We did as best as we could, the tar is safe inside the walls. However, Gaspar was and is relentless. I fear that it is no longer safe outside these doors. I have never known a Lord to kill his own father and relentlessly hunt one person, as he hunts you dear Lady. I would ask that Ruby and I be allowed to stay until this is over. I fear for my wife, but I fear more of what would happen if Gasper were to get his hands on my daughter." Lord Baron told his tale in a haunted voice. Raven was shocked all she could think about was her dream.

"Do you think Gasper will allow the other chiefs to return? Or is he too far gone?" She heard Krystopher ask. Waiting to hear Lord Baron reply, Raven said

"Yes lord, you and Ruby are very welcome to stay. As are your remaining guards. Do you think my brother would allow a massager through so that you could contact your family and let them know what is going on?"

"Unfortunately, I don't think that he will allow anyone out, if you are lucky, he will allow the servants to come and go from the keep. However, he will watch and count all who enter and leave. He may even detain them to make sure none of us leave. I just do not know my Lady as I said before only an insane man would attack during this time of year instead of readying his clan for winter." Lord Baron said very tiredly.

"You should go find your bed Lord Baron, Lord Krystopher and I will be finding our own beds soon as well."

He did not have to be told twice, he rose and slowly made his way up the stairs to the guest quarters. Raven and Krystopher did not say anything until they heard the door shut.

"Well, what do you think my friend?" Raven asked as she turned her attention to Krystopher, who had been very quiet.

"I fear that we have been betrayed. Don't look at me in horror. Think about it your brother waits until everyone has left then he attacks. Draco did not warn anyone of Gaspar's presence. Now a couple of things can interfere with wolf magic, one is, it is suppressed through a tonic and the other is if it is being blocked. Do you know of anyone that Draco would trust without thought or question?"

"Other than his family no." Raven said after thinking about it Krystopher excused himself and went to bed. Raven sat for a bit longer at the table deep in thought. It was well after midnight before she found her bed. Yet sleep still eluded her as her mind continually went over who would profit from betraying Azure and his clan not to mention who would profit from her death.

Chapter 19

Raven was going stir crazy. She had become so used to practicing and going outside every day that being shut up in the keep for 2 weeks straight was driving her mad. Azure would meet behind closed doors every day with Krystopher and Lord Baron. Gaspar had dug in around the outer walls of the keep, he had a rather large size force with him every few days Raven would hear from the young man she had saved about how half of Gasper's camp left only to be replaced by the same number of fresh men. Gaspar never allowed anyone in or out of the keep without first asking them who they were and what they were doing. He only allowed twenty people in a day, and no one was allowed to bring in any outside supplies. Fortunately, the keep had a good supply of food laid in for the winter.

One morning, Raven awoke before Azure and dressed in her practice cloths of leather pants and a loose tunic. As she headed out the door of her room, she grabbed her wooden sword and headed to the main hall. She saw Ruby and Draco sitting together with their heads very close whispering. Draco had become distant since Gaspar have invaded. Raven had tried to talk to him several times, but he would always come up with some excuse and leave. She brought it up to Azure a couple of times, but he would wave her off as being too overprotective of the boy. Ruby saw her and asked.

"Are you going outside to practice Lady Raven? I was under the impression that none, but servants may leave the hall?"

"No, Ruby I am going to practice right here in the great hall. You are welcome to join me if you want, you as well Draco. All we need to do is move the long table over to the side and we will have plenty of room." Raven responded as she placed her sword on the table and began pushing the solid oak benches over to the side of the room. She heard running footsteps and looked up to see Ruby dashing up the stairs. She went back to moving the bench. Before she had one all the way over against the wall, she was joined by two of the guards. Ruby was changed and back downstairs before the second bench was in place against the wall. It took Raven, Ruby, the two guards and two more guards to move the table out of the way. The smaller tables and benches around the room were quickly and easily moved.

"Do you have a second wooden sword Lady Raven? I don't have one and I would greatly enjoy learning how to use a sword." Ruby said almost shyly. Before Raven could respond Draco was handing Ruby a wooden sword. Raven noticed that Oryeon and Beo were with him with their wooden swords as well. It was not long before they were all sparing in the great hall. Even a few guards joined in with wooded swords as well. The hall quickly was filled with the sounds of wood on wood hitting, occasionally the constant sound was broken by a shout of "UNFAIR!" or, "NOT ALLOWED!"

The maids brought food in from the kitchen for everyone to break their fast as they wished. Raven was sparing with Ruby when all of a sudden Azure's mother shouted.

"WHAT IS GOING ON HERE!!!!!" The hall went silent.

"My apologies My Lady Leena it was my idea to spar in the main hall." Raven said with her head held high.

"I see, Lady Raven and what does your Husband have to say about this? I do not see him about." She responded coldly as she walked to were Raven stood.

"I left him sleeping in our bed, my Lady I awoke and needed to practice."

"I see and who gave the guards permission to join in?" She looked at the guards in utter disgust as if they had been playing with toys instead of sparing.

"I saw no harm is allowing them to spar with us my Lady when I was asked. Even your own children spar, in fact Draco is teaching young Ruby how to fight."

"I see well since it has already happened, I have no ground on which to say no. I only ask that you teach your mother and I how to fight as well. Especially with both of us without mates now, we should know how to defend ourselves. Since our guards are so easily distracted." She again glared at the guards.

"Fair enough my Lady I would suggest that you change out of your dress and into a pair of breeches and tunic. I believe that the guards would be better suited to teach your Ladyship in the ways of sword fighting as I will be busy with my mother." Raven said smugly the look on Lady Leena's face was a cross between shock and outrage. However, Leena turned on her heel and headed towards the direction of her room. Raven then asked a maid to fetch her mother and have her wear clothes that she could practice in. She also asked that the maid stop and pick up a practice sword for her mother to use. Raven turned to the guards who were looking anywhere but at her, they seemed slightly embarrassed.

"I am asking for a volunteer to train Lady Leena. You all heard what she said and saw what she thinks of you sparing in the great hall. I will not force any of you to teach her." As she spoke, she looked at every guard as if she was talking just to them.

"I will teach the Lady Leena do not fear my friend." Krystopher said from behind Raven. Blushing at the fact that she did not even know he was there she turned slowly. He was wearing homespun pants and a tunic, in his hand he carried two wooden swords. Before she could say anything, she saw her mother at the top of the stairs. She was wearing woolen pants and a woolen shirt both of which were the chestnut in color. She carried her sword like she knew how to use it.

Raven waited for her mother while the other went back to sparing. "You seem to know how to use that mother"

"Yes, your father taught me shortly after we were married. I must admit that I am out of practice. However, don't go easy on me I need to remember everything. I spend every day in fear of your bastard brother attacking." With that the two women began sparing.

By the time Azure came down to the main hall it was once more ringing with the dull wooden sounds of sparing. Lady Leena still had not joined the group, so Krystopher challenged Azure to a sparring match. Azure was very happy to accommodate him. Everyone cleared the center of the room to allow the two of them to spare. The two men held nothing back not strength and not speed. It was just a blur of movement and the sound of wood hitting wood. Two hours later Raven had enough and called for a cease. The men separated and all spectators could see that both men were dripping sweat. Their cloths were wet, and the solid maple wooden swords had major dents in them.

"Do you feel better love?" Raven asked as she walked over to her husband.

"Yes, I do. How about you Krystopher do you feel better?" Azure asked with a laugh in his voice.

Before he could respond a servant came rushing in with her dress practically in tatters. She fell at Raven and Azure's feet sobbing.

"Forgive me, my Lord and Lady. I had no choice he has my son." The woman was sobbing uncontrollably. Raven knelt beside her to try and console her. The next thing Raven knew she was on her back and the servant was at her throat with a blade.

"Come near me and she dies this is a silver dagger harmless to humans but from what my lover tells me just a scratch is deadly to your kind. You think you are so much better than all of us because you spawn from wolves. Well, my lover spawned from your kind and he hates that part of him. Once his sister is dead then he will be free of his curse, and we can be together. HAHAHA" she reared back and began a downward arc towards Raven's stomach as she laughed hysterically.

Raven shoved the woman off her and grappled with her to get the dagger away from the crazy woman. Raven quickly got the upper hand, and she banged the woman's head against the floor until she stopped moving and her eyes rolled up into her skull. Fear gripped Raven's heart a fear that she had killed the woman. Raven felt her neck for a heartbeat she found a very strong one and felt a wave of relief. Two guards lifted the woman off the floor and took her to the dungeon.

Raven saw Arian walk towards her and help her up off the floor and then her mother ushering her towards the stairs. As she reached the top, she heard Azure call all the servants to the main hall. Raven spent the next two days sequestered in her room refusing to allow any one in, even her husband. She was so mortified by what she had almost done. She was raised to honor human life not to end it. Of course, she knew how to make the deep sleep tinctures, that the very old or the critically injured would ask Key-Na to make for them when they were too tired to go on. But Key-Na had taught her that it was the person's choice, she just gave them the tool. Animals were raised for food or clothing but even then, you did not take what you could not use.

How would she ever be able to fight against her brother, who was so set on killing her that he just had a servant, his supposed lover, try and kill her? He was so evil Raven wondered if it would just be better to have him kill her and end this war before it started. Then the memory of her father's bloody broken body flashed in her mind. With that memory firmly in the front of her mind she hardened her heart against her brother. He was no longer anything to her other than a tyrant. With her resolve she threw back her shoulder and walked out of her room. She found Azure in the hall surrounded by papers. He looked haggard and had perplexed look on his face.

"What are you doing my husband?" Raven saw Azure's eyes lit up when he looked up and saw her. He stood up long enough to kiss her and then sat back down heavily, as if the weight of all the world was on his shoulders.

"Trying to research how Draco's abilities are not working and who that crazy woman was. After you went upstairs, I gathered all the servants together no one was missing, and no one knew who she was. To prevent that from happening again all the servant have a phrase that they say each morning to the guards. It will slow things down because each servant must say it there will be 10 guards that operate the front gate. If a servant does not know the phrase, then someone that knows them may vouch for them or they will be turned away. The phrase changes each night before the servants leave that was Krystopher's idea. He has something to ask of you, you can find him out on the practice field. I have lifted the ban on anyone going out of the keep, my concern was that someone would climb the wall and kill you or someone else precious to me. The walls are all that protect us from your madman of a brother. However, someone did walk in here and attack us. Also, Mother has banned all sparing in the great hall, claiming that all the noise was giving her a horrid headache." At that he bent his head and began looking over his papers again.

Raven left him to his papers and headed towards the kitchen where some of the best scents she had ever smelled were wafting out. She recognized the Honey cakes and the smell of the sweet herb bread that she loved. Nara and her children were in the kitchen they seemed in good spirits despite everything happening.

"Nara, you look to be in a good mood as do the children."

"Oh, Lady Raven I did not see you there. I have some fresh Honey cakes if you would like one. Yes, I am in a good mood, Krystopher asked me this morning if it would be alright if he asked Lady Leena if the children and I could stay in the keep. I did not realize how gentle a man he is." Raven noticed that Nara said the last part with a loving tone.

"I see, well I am going to go talk with him is there anything you would like me to bring him?" Raven asked, Nara's face grew scarlet in color.

"Um......No Lady Raven." She said as she turned her full attention to the dough that she was working. Raven grabbed a honey cake and headed out the back door of the kitchen. She found Krystopher and Lord Baron sparring together. They were well matched but Azure and Krystopher had been deadly in their focus. Raven ate her Honey cake and waited for the combatants to break apart before she cleared her throat.

"Krystopher, you wanted to talk to me." She called across the yard. He looked at her and waved his hand. He turned back to Lord Baron handed him the wooden practice sword and shook his hand. He walked quickly over to Raven.

"Hello, my Lady, yes I have a question for you. What is the long-term support that you want me to give Nara and her children?"

"Krystopher, I told you that you had to provide and take care of them for 6 months. What you do after that time is up to you and Nara to decide. Why do you ask? Do the two of not get along? Will it be difficult for you to be around her for 6 months?"

"No, nothing like that. I want her in my life, I want her for my mate. I am just not sure how to approach her about it. I mean she knows that I killed her husband and yet she still is willing to talk to me and be around me. She makes me laugh my Lady. She makes me feel alive, do I have the right to ask her to be my mate?" Raven could feel the desperation in Krystopher's voice, he seemed confused totally different that his normal confident self.

"Talk to her. Asking permission for her and the children to stay in the keep is a good first step. Hopefully after Gasper is handled things will settle down and you two can focus on each other. Now I am going to head in and challenge Azure to a game of chess." Raven gave his arm a slight squeeze and headed into the great hall.

Raven spent the rest of the day playing chess with Azure as well as playing a couple of games with Beo. Raven realized that Azure was not kidding when he said that Beo had a mind for strategies. That night at dinner Raven watched Krystopher and Nara with the children sit together. They all seemed happy, when Raven asked about it after dinner Nara told her that Lady Leena had agreed to allow them to stay in the keep as Krystopher's guests. They didn't need anything from their home, so they did not have to leave.

Chapter 20

For the next two days Raven and the other women of the keep worked on mixing the tar, pitch, and resin together and putting it into the gourds. The following day after midday meal Raven saw the woman that had tried to attack her. Azure sat himself and Raven at the head of the great table, once they were seated, he signaled the guards to bring the prisoner into the main hall. The woman's hand were bound behind her back and the guards lead her around with a rope at her neck.

"You stand before us accused of attempted murder. How do you plead?" Azure asked from his seat at the head of the table. Raven watched her raised her head as if she was looking down her nose at everyone and clearly said.

"What I did was out of love. When I attacked your harlot of a wife and poisoned your brother. I did it all out of love. Once you are all gone, he will be free of his curse." As she said the last word she began to laugh hysterically.

"What do you mean poisoning my brother how?" Azure asked forcefully. She stopped laughing long enough to say

"I have been putting Wolf's Bane in his food for weeks now. My lover will win over everyone…"before she could say anything else Lady Leena had rushed through the crowd and attacked the woman. It took a few moments before anyone reacted by the time the guards pulled her off the servant there was only a bloody mess of ropes clothing and misshapen things on the floor. Raven looked at Lady Leena's hands and saw that her fingers were elongated, and each had a claw on the end of it. As the guard held her, she began to cry. Raven and Arian both walked towards Lady Leena. They each supported an arm and the three of them walked to Lady Leena's rooms. The stairs were a little bit difficult, but they managed without anyone falling.

Lady Leena kept silently crying the whole way. Raven was surprised at the starkness of Lady Leena's rooms. There was no color anywhere it was all bare stone, the blanket on the bed was just as grey as the stones. The fireplace looked as if it had not been used in several days. The women gently laid Lady Leena down on her bed, Raven went over to make a fire, but her mother placed her hand on her arm and shook her head. They both walked back out of the room. By the time the two of them walked back into the main hall everyone was gone and maids were working hard on scrubbing the floor. Raven walked with her mother over to where their cloaks hung by the front door. Once they were on the two of them headed outside for a bit it had snowed sometime during the night.

"Mother, I am at a loss for what to do about Gasper. I would greatly appreciate any counsel you could give me. I would like to speak in my room to avoid others over hearing."

"Of course, but can we please stay out here a bit longer. I have been stuck in the keep for far too long." Arian asked as she turned to walk away across the courtyard. Raven and her mother walked around the courtyard for a bit avoiding the practice area. Raven saw Ruby and Draco sparing along with several others included Azure, Oryeon, and Beo. Azure was sparing against both of his brothers Raven stopped to watch the three of them spar. She felt her mother beside her turn and start heading back inside. She turned and hurried to catch up with her mother.

As they approached the main doors, they heard a scuffle behind them. They turned hearing a high pitch scream. Raven saw Ruby fall to her knees next to a body that was on the practice field. Raven and her mother rushed over to see what happened. They saw Draco laying on the ground the snow around him turning red.

"Ruby how did this happen? All the practice swords are dulled so not to draw blood." Raven was turn over Draco on his back so she could see his wound. There was a large, jagged cut across his stomach like someone had tried to disembowel him. She whipped her cloak off and began pressing it on the wound.

"I don't know what happened one moment we were sparing, and Draco was giving me directions. The next moment someone said his name he turned, and a guard slashed him across the stomach. He fell right away and that was when I screamed. Please Lady Raven help him." She was crying as she told Raven what happened. By the time Ruby stopped talking Azure was on the ground next to his brother helping Raven try and stop the blood flow. Raven looked at Azure and saw stark fear on his face.

"Mother, we need Cor right now and someone find that guard that did this!" She heard footsteps run off, but she did not dare look up from her task. Raven was having a hard time slowing the blood.

"Azure, gather up some clean snow I saw some by the wall. Ruby, I need you to focus and run inside to get some cloth to help with this bleeding and have the maids get my healing supplies ready." She helped pack Draco's wound with snow the cold helped slow the bleeding. Ruby came back with the cloths and told Raven that the maids were doing what they were asked.

"The bleeding has slowed down enough we can move him inside. Guards help me slide some spears under him to keep him flat as possible. It will take all of us to move him inside." Raven said in her most commanding voice

"Stop everyone!! All guard take off your helms right now I will only allow those of you I know to come in." Azure said in a commanding voice. All the guard immediately removed their helms and fell to a knee. Raven saw her mother in wolf form walking around the practice yard. As she watched her mother, she heard Azure picking a handful of guards. They carefully slid long spears under Draco. Two of the spears formed an x under Draco and the other two stayed straight. Everyone rose at once, to make it so that Raven could keep pressure on the wound. It was slow going getting into the keep. She glanced back once to try and find her mother, but she had disappeared.

They gently set down Draco on the table and removed the spears before Raven began to work in earnest. She was so focused that she was startled when Cor stepped in to help. It took hours to fix all the damage even with Cor and Raven both working on him. They were both exhausted once they were done. Raven covered Draco with his favorite bear pelt that Ruby gathered for him, from his room. Azure helped Raven sit down on a bench and sat down next to her. She watched Krystopher help Cor sit down by the fire. She could see that Cor's skin had an ashen color to it and he was shaking slightly. Ruby grabbed Draco's hand and sat down on the bench next to the table to begin a vigil.

"Will he survive? Should we move him?" Azure asked in a hushed voice.

"With luck and rest he should recover well enough; he will always have a dull pain and a vicious scar. While we were cleaning the wound, I noticed that there had been other damage to his organs. I am afraid that when we find the one who attacked him, we will have to thank them before we execute them. The servant girl was telling the truth." Raven heard Azure release a low growl upon hearing the extent of damage to his brother. "As for moving him, I would rather have him immobile for as long as possible. I know that we heal fast, but he needs to stay still to heal properly. He also needs to stay warm."

"Why do you say we will have to thank them?" Azure asked with shock in his voice.

"Because without the attack, I would not know how bad the poisoning was. He will have to be treated with hot mead and bread for a while, but he should be fine. That is why I said we have to thank his assassin. I am so tired husband, please help me to bed." Azure helped her stand and walked with her to the stairs. As they passed Ruby, Raven gently laid her hand on the girl shoulder and gave a small squeeze. As they approached the stairs the door was opened, and a snowy gust of wind blew through the hall. Raven's mother padded in on silent paws and headed towards the stairs.

"Did you find the traitor Lady Arian?" Azure asked the wolf nodded her head and the bounded up the stairs. Raven knew that she needed to stay awake to hear what her mother had found but she was too exhausted. At Azure's urging she walked to their room and laid down.

"I know that you are very tired love. However, I cannot sleep right now I have to discover what your mother found out."

Raven responded barely above a whisper "Go I will be fine." The last thing she heard was the door closing. Raven awoke from the nightmare screaming and crying, it was the same dream again. She realized that she was in Azure's arms.

"Tell me what happened my love." He asked in a pleading voice.

"I had the same dream as before. I fear that if we attack Rose Hedge where he has the advantage, we will not survive." Raven was shaking so bad that she was afraid that she would shake apart. Azure held her through out the rest of the night it was dawn before Raven was able to fall back asleep. It was midday before Raven woke up again. She was alone in the room as she sat up, she saw a beautiful long sleeved green dress laying at the foot of the bed.

She dressed quickly and headed downstairs eager to hear what her mother found the night before. She did not have to look very far her mother was sitting next to Leena beside the fireplace. Her mother lifted her face and looked at Raven her face breaking into a smile. Lady Leena continued to stare at the fire.

"Raven, I was afraid that you wouldn't wake up until dinner. Azure told me that you had the dream again. Do you really think if the attack happens it will not end well?" Raven walked over to the women.

"I do not know mother. Lady Leena it is good to see you. How is Draco fairing?" Raven asked as she knelt in front of Lady Leena.

"My son sleeps, your mother gave him a tea to help keep him asleep while he heals. Ruby will not leave his side. Azure said that you saw how much the wolf's bane damaged his organs. Please tell me will I lose my son?" Lady Leena's voice was broken as tears streamed down her face. She clasped Raven's hands, Raven could feel how cold the Lady's hands were and how they shook slightly.

"My dear Lady, Draco will survive both his wound and the damage from the poison. He will never be as strong as he could have been, had he not suffered either. May I suggest that you and Arian go for a walk around the grounds. You need fresh air, worrying over Draco and not taking care of yourself will do no one any good. Mother would you please grab Lady Leena's cloak and go on a walk with her? I take it you told Azure of what you found last night?" Raven asked as she stood up and looked at her mother. Arian nodded before walking over to the main doors. Raven helped Lady Leena stand and walked with her over to her mother.

"Mother, do you know where Azure is?"

"Yes, he said something at morning meal about being up on the wall overlooking the side gate today. He was going to be there until dinner. Why do you ask?"

"I will go talk to him after I have some food. I just want to know what you found out last night and I think that Lady Leena needs you more than I do right now. Oh, please don't look at me like that, I will ask Azure now go for a walk please mother." Arian nodded and both her and Lady Leena walked out the door. Raven watched as a couple of guards feel in beside them. She closed the door and headed to the kitchen to find some food. She found some bread and a bit of cheese. She pulled up a chair to the counter and sat enjoying the simple fair.

"Lady Raven, why are you in the kitchen is something amiss?" Raven heard a gruff male voice come from behind her. She jumped and spun so fast that the chair fell and hit the floor. She was looking at a man she had never seen before. He was older and very lean his hair was salt and peppered from age.

"Who are you?" She asked trying to remember everything that she had been taught about fighting from Azure. The man held up his hands as if to show her that he was harmless.

"I am Joel the butcher. I normally am not at the keep. It was butchering day yesterday in the village. The head cook Mary likes to have a large roast the day after, however I came to tell her that a lot of the meat was stolen last night. Unless there is a hunt soon, we will not have enough meat for winter."

"What do you mean stolen, did you tell Lady Leena or anyone else?"

"No, my Lady I was trying to find Mary first. I knew she would know who to inform. However, I have not been able to find her. Have you seen her?" Raven relaxed a bit at his explanation.

"No, I am afraid that I overslept today, and I have not seen her. I will go talk to Lord Azure and find out what is to be done. Please stay here do not leave this room." She said as she walked over to the back door of the kitchen and opened it. As she walked through the garden, she was silently kicking herself for not grabbing a cloak before walking outside. She looked around for her mother and Lady Leena as she walked to the side gate but did not see them anywhere.

Once she reached the side gate she called up to Azure.

"Azure are you up there?" she waited and was rewarded with him looking over the battlement.

"Raven what are you doing out here without a cloak. You will catch your death of cold. Stay there I will be right there." Raven waited rubbing her hands up and down her arms in hopes of warming up. She did not have to wait long before Azure was standing in front of her wrapping her up in his heavy bear hide cloak.

"Thank you love," Raven said as she deeply inhaled Azure's scent.

"Now my love why are you out here?" He asked with such concern in his voice

"I was in the kitchen when I was startled by a man. He claims his name is Joel and that he is the butcher. He was looking for Mary do you know this man?"

"Joel? Yes, I know him I wonder why he was looking for Mary."

"Well according to him a lot of meat was stolen last night after the day of butchering. He wanted to talk to Mary; to one let her know that unless there is a hunt soon there will not be enough meat for winter and two, to find out who he needed to talk to about the theft."

"I see well. We have a problem then. Alright let's go find my mother and inform her of the theft." Azure said as he put his arm around Raven's shoulders and started heading to the main hall. Once inside Azure hung his cloak up on one of the pegs by the door then they both walked over to the fireplace to warm up.

"That is odd I thought that my mother would be here by the fire." Azure said as they warmed up

"Her and Arian went for a walk. By the way why did you decide to let the guards have their helmets back on after what happened last night?" Raven asked looking at him

"Raven what do you mean? The guards still do not have their helmets on." If Raven was not looking at Azure's face, she would not have seen him pale.

"I saw two guards with their helmets on fall into step with our mothers as they walked out the door. I thought that you had let them have their helmets back." Raven felt a knot of dread form in her stomach. As one they turned and rushed up the stairs. Raven ran to her mother's room only to find it empty. She met up with Azure in the hall coming from his mother's room. He shook his head at her.

"Maybe they are in the kitchen." Raven said hopefully. They rushed towards the kitchen however before they got there, they heard a shout from the front door.

"LORD AND LADY COME QUICK!" They froze in their tracks and looked; it was the young man that Raven had healed. Seeing him made her realize something very bad had happened. She ran to the door remembering at the last second to grab a cloak from the pegs. She heard

Azure a half step behind her as they ran behind the young man. He took them up the stairs at the front gate. Once at the top, he pointed over the battlements and Raven's heart froze in her chest. Standing there in the middle of the village was Gasper he had both Arian and Leena standing there in their undergarments bound with silver chains. Raven could tell they were silver by the way her mother's and Lady Leena's bodies where bright red everywhere the chain connected.

"How did this happen?" Azure asked in a deadly calm voice. Raven heard the young man swallow loudly and he said.

"It was my fault my lord. I saw Lady Arian and Lady Leena walking with four guards. The guards said that you had given the Ladies permission to walk to town because we had not seen Gasper or his army for a couple of days. I knew that Lady Arian had caught and killed the assassin last night, so I did not think to question I just opened the gate." Raven could hear the anguish in his confession. Before Azure could say anything, a man approached the gates waving a white flag. Raven recognized him as Jerome, Gasper's man servant. She turned and told Azure who it was walking to the gate.

"I have terms for Lord Azure." He shouted once he was at the gates. Azure looked over the battlement into the courtyard and nodded his head. Raven heard the gates open, and she looked over the battlement at Jerome. She saw him hand something to a guard he then turned and walked back towards the village. The guard brought the rolled-up paper up to Azure. Raven read over his shoulder.

I know all about your plan and I have to say it might have worked. Here are my terms One unconditional surrender, two you and that woman are banished for all time, three the Wolf Soul clan convinces all the other clans to name me sole leader. If these terms are not met all will die starting with your mothers.

Lord Gasper chief of the Wolf Tear clan soon to be chief of the Five Clans.

"He is insane. What are we going to do?" Raven asked in a very distraught voice.

"We are not going to do anything love. I am going to challenge him here and now." Azure said with a tone that did not broke any argument. They walked hand in hand down into the courtyard.

"I will not stay here behind these walls while you are fighting him. I stand with you we live together, or we die together. Write a letter naming Krystopher leader of the clan until one of the boys can take over. He will take them somewhere safe; Gasper can't stay in the village much longer winter is almost here, he will have to go home. Let us face him as a united front please husband." Raven's voice was far steadier than she felt. After a moment Azure nodded his head and they hurried into the keep. The plan was while Raven located Krystopher, Azure wrote a letter stating that Krystopher was in charge of the clan until one of the triples came of age.

Raven found Krystopher and Nara in the sewing room along with the children. At the quick glance that Raven cast about many women where in the room all working on different projects. Raven called Krystopher out of the room.

"Krystopher, I need you to come with me right now. Do you know where the boys are?"

"I think they had planed on spending time with Draco. Why, what has happened?"

"I will explain as we walk but we must hurry." She turned and began walking quickly back to where she hoped Azure was. She gave as brief and explanation as she could as they walked. They found Azure finishing the letter in the main hall.

"Did Raven tell you what has happened?"

"Yes, she has told me. Lord Azure I do not know how I will get the boys safely out of here." Raven had not heard Krystopher sound so upset before.

"Be clam Krystopher, in the cellar behind the largest barrel is a secret passage it exits well outside of the village. Walk four more days to the east and you will come to Lord Baron's lands. You should be safe there, as far as I know he does not know that Lord Baron is still here. Show him the letter he will help you. If we are not back before nightfall leave, this is not a request. You can find him in the library at the end of the hall he is fond of books so that is where he spends his days. I will not say goodbye to my brothers. Come love, let us go met our fate." Azure said as he held out his hand for hers. Raven placed her hand in his and held her head up high as they walked out of the keep.

At the gate he signaled the guards to open the gate. Raven felt like every part of her was shaking but she continued to walk beside Azure. She hoped they came out of this alive, but she knew that it was possible that they would die. Guards flanked them when they were out of the keep. They wore Azure's clans' armor, but she had a feeling that they were not of his clan. Then a spark of genius or insanity stuck she was not sure which. Gasper was still standing in the road both Lady Leena and Lady Arian were on the ground Raven could see their faces matching masks of pain.

"Gasper, I challenge you for the right to rule the Wolf Tear Clan as is my right by wolf law being first born. Do you accept or do you yield?" Raven said when they were close enough that she knew her brother would hear her.

"You? You a wolf that cannot even change, is challenging me a wolf in his prime? You are choosing death very well. Once I dispatch you, I will have no one to challenge me. Very well, I accept your challenge." Gasper said his voice grating on Raven's nerves.

"Raven, what the hell do you think you are doing?! I challenge you in her place!" Azure shouted to Gasper. She briefly glanced over her shoulder and saw four guards holding Azure on his knee in the street. His face had a look of pure fear on. She turned back to face her brother before her heart broke at the look on Azure's face.

"Oh, do not fear I will kill you as well. You will just watch her die first. Then watch your mother's die, then your brothers and lastly you." Gasper said to Azure a sneer in his voice.

"I ask that you be checked for silver before we fight. I think only then could our clan guards whole heartedly accept you as the leader of the Wolf Tear Clan. I will even submit to a search to prove that the challenge was fair.

"I agree sister." He said sister with such hatred that Raven felt it as a slap across her face.

"Be sure to check his teeth the first time he attached me he had a sliver of silver in his tooth." Her statement had the effect she wanted; she saw some of the guards look at each other with a look of surprise on their faces.

"One last thing Gasper while we are searched, why did you kill our father?" Raven heard a collective gasp from the guards. Raven saw Jerome walk over to Gasper and she heard him asked.

"My Lord is this true? Did you commit patricide? Did you kill the chief?" She could hear the worry in his voice.

"He was not my father after he chose her! He was no longer chief after I claimed he was dead by her hand! NOW SILENCE JEROME!" There was a growl as he shouted. He shoved Jerome away. Raven had no time to react she was slammed into by a grey humanoid wolf. Fortunately, she was smaller than him and she managed to wiggle out from under him. She quickly shed her cloak and ran towards a guard. He held his hands up as if to silently say 'I cannot help you' Raven rolled her eyes at him and unsheathed his sword. She spun and brought the sword to block as Gasper swung his large hairy clawed arm at her.

Raven knew that she would not be able to fight him like this for long. Her plan had been to dodge and perry his attacks to ware him out before she shifted. She had not factored in the strength behind the attacks. That one block had sent vibrations up her arm, she had to think of something quickly. She dodged another arm swing and dashed behind him. As she ran behind him, she sliced at his leg, hoping to cut the tendon that ran up the back of the leg. She had not planned on the sword being so dull and his hide being so tough.

She turned to face him again quickly backing up to put space between them. She heard a scuffle behind her, but she did not dare take her eyes off of Gasper. His eyes blazed red with hatred for her. She brought the sword up again and tried to slash at his eyes. He batted the sword away with such force that it knocked her off her feet. He dropped to all four legs and stalked towards her; she called the wolf at the same time she tore at her dress.

The wolf answered her call. They melded together; it was so fast that Raven almost didn't move quick enough to miss her brother biting at her throat. She stood up it was then that she fully realized that she was a humanoid wolf like him. He stopped in his tracks Raven saw his nose scenting the air. The world erupted in chaos there were too many scents and too much sound. Raven tried to force the wolf to focus on Gasper, but she had never been in this form before. Gasper hit her hard and low driving his shoulder into her stomach.

She was on the ground again and she felt his teeth bite into her neck, she could feel that they were close to touching. In a last-ditch effort, she brought her clawed hands up and raked deep across his face. He released her with a howl of pain blood flowing down his snout from where she had raked his eyes. She laid there in the road her throat torn she knew she would die there but, she had to end his life. With the last bit of her strength, she lunged for him digging both clawed hands into his stomach. She used one hand tearing and clawing the muscles and lungs reaching for his heart, her other hand she shredded his other organs. She was losing blood fast as her hand closed around the vital pumping organ. She pulled her hand out still gripping his heart ripping it out of his chest she felt herself fall before she hit the road, she crushed his heart in her hand. Her last thought was that she had not told Azure she loved him before she challenged her brother.

Chapter 21

Raven was very confused she should be dead and yet she wasn't, she could feel her body. Her throat ached and something heavy was laying on her arm. She opened her eyes she was in a room it was dimly lit from the low burning fire in the fireplace. She tried to turn her head, but her neck was held in place somehow. She tried to talk but all that came out was a hushed whisper. It was enough; however, she felt the bed shift and then Azure's face was looming over her. Raven saw tears in his eyes, she drew her brows together in a silent question.

"We will talk in the morning go back to sleep my love. I am so glad that you finally woke up. You do need more sleep to heal." Raven felt Azure gently hug her and then she fell back to sleep with his arms around her.

It was morning when Raven woke up again. She could tell that Azure was not in the bed she could hear the fire crackle and pop. For some reason she still could not move her head. Raven was becoming distressed at her inability to move her head, as she went to move her arm, she discovered that she could not even move her arms. Her panic was mounting she could not move at all.

She heard the door open she let out a raspy breath in an attempt to talk. She heard rushing footsteps and then Azure was leaning over her. She knew she had panic in her eyes.

"Calm yourself love. You were very badly injured; it took Cor and I both working on you to get you stable enough for your mother to help. Before you hurt yourself listen to me. I will tell you everything that has happened. I am going to sit you up not much but, enough to get some food into you." He leaned down and much like one would with a child he placed his hands under her arms and lifted her into a sitting position. True to his word it was not very much but it was enough for her to realize that a lot of time had passed. The night gown that she was wearing was very loose on her. She followed Azure with her eyes, and he stoked the fire and brought a bowl with steam wafting off of it to the bed. He sat down on the bed and began to spoon the broth into Raven's mouth. She was glad to know that her mouth opened and closed however it hurt a lot to swallow.

"I know it hurts love, but I need you to try. So, while you eat, I will tell you everything. You have been unconscious for almost 3 months. Winter is fully upon us; the snows are some of the worst I have seen. It seems everyday it we have at least 3 feet added to what was already on the ground. Where to start it has been hard, harder than anything I have even had to deal with. Here have just a bit more broth. I will start with the last thing you remember. The challenge between you and your brother. While you fought Gasper, Jerome realized that he had lost his mind. With Gasper distracted Jerome freed Arian and Leena, he ordered the guards to let me go. We were going to intervene when you pulled your stunt. I did not know you knew how to blend. Gasper had taken Cor a couple of days before Jerome released him before the fight was even done. Between Cor's healing abilities and my time manipulation we managed to keep you here. It was a long fight we spent most of a month healing you. When we were too tired to use our magic, your mother would use healing herbs to try and help. Joel with Jerome's help recovered the stolen meat. We also found out it had been Mary who was helping your brother sneak people in. He was her grandson, no one even knew here. She told my father a sob story after Gasper was a teenager about how she needed a place to stay. When she found out that he was here she decided that she had to help him. She is currently in the dungeon awaiting our ruling. Draco has healed. Lord Baron along with Ruby and him left last month in hopes of beating the snow. I received a messenger this morning stating that they had made it safe. Cor figures it will take a while before you are able to eat on your own and even longer before you can talk. The reason you can't move on your own is because you haven't moved for such a long time. It will take time Cor is hoping that by the time winter is over you will be more like yourself. Krystopher is currently in charge of Rose Hedge until you are well enough to travel. I can see that you are tired we can talk more later. One last thing we burned Gasper's body a day after the fight. Well in reality Jerom burned his body while Cor and I were focused on healing you. Now go back to sleep I will not be far." He slid her back under the blankets and she fell asleep slowly going over all the information that Azure had given her.

The rest of the winter past slowly for Raven. Cor would come and visited her every day to check on her healing progress. Her mother would visit as would Lady Leena neither of them seemed bothered by the fact that Raven could not talk, she got the impression that they just did not want to be alone. She wasn't allowed to leave her room per Cor's orders. So, most days after she was able to walk, she would sit by the fire with a book from the library. Beo and Oryeon both visited her. Beo brought a chess set during one of his visits, Raven was happy to have something to do other than read. Once she was able to talk. Azure and her decided that Mary would be given a choice swear fidelity to Azure or be banished. Azure inform Raven that Mary had chosen banishment. Fortunately, Nara had stayed behind when Krystopher left for Rose Hedge. So the keep had a cook, once Mary left.

By the time spring came around Raven, was almost back to normal she walked with minimal problems and her throat was healed enough that as long as she did not raise her voice, she could talk all day. She received a messenger from Krystopher informing her that he was more than ready to hand her clan back to her. He had other more important things to take care of also he would see her soon. True to his word four days later Krystopher came riding into the courtyard at Oakheart. Raven and Cor were out walking in the courtyard when Krystopher rode in.

"Cor where do you think would be the best place for a medicinal herb garden should be?" Raven asked as they walked around.

"Well, I am not sure I…. Hello cousin." Cor rushed over to see Krystopher, Raven followed at a slower pace. She was happy to see the cousins together again.

"Welcome back Krystopher, I am sure that Nara with be very happy to see you. Now come down here and give me a hug before you rush off to see her, she is in the kitchen." Raven said with a chuckle in her voice. Krystopher quickly dismounted and gave Raven a very large hug lifting her off her feet. He swung her around once and then set her down and bounded off to the kitchen's back door. Raven heard very clearly when he surprised Nara.

"Well Cor, I think we should head inside and find out what has Krystopher in such a good mood over." Raven said over her shoulder as she made her way to the main door for the keep. Raven walked over to where Azure had been sitting talking with his captain of the guards. Raven saw his eyes shined with love when he saw her. She walked over and stood behind him placing her hand on his shoulder. He reached his hand up and covered hers.

"Thank you, Captain, I will think on what you have suggested." Azure said in a dismissive tone. The captain stood up and walked away. Azure pulled Raven around to in front of him and down into his lap. He was nuzzling her neck when there was a loud whoop from the kitchen. Before they could stand Krystopher came out holding Nara in his arms.

"SHE SAID YES!" Krystopher shouted at the top of his lungs. Raven feeling how happy he was began to laugh from his joy.

"Well then we will have a double reason to celebrate." Azure said still sitting holding Raven in his lap "I received a message this morning from Lord Baron, Draco and Ruby are engaged to be married when they come of age."

"Oh, Azure that is wonderful." Raven said as she flung her arms around his neck. Raven felt that her life would not be any more complete than it was in that moment.

www.ingramcontent.com/pod-product-compliance
Lightning Source LLC
Chambersburg PA
CBHW061352310726
48974CB00001B/305